Danny's Bed

A Tale of Ghosts and Poltergeists In Savannah, Georgia

is a publication of Whitaker Street Press
346 Whitaker Street
Savannah, Georgia 31401
by
Al Cobb

FRONT COVER PHOTO - AL COBB

Copyright 2000
This publication may not be copied, reproduced or transmitted by any means, in part or in whole without the prior written consent of the publisher.
ISBN: 0-9705537-0-6
Library of Congress Catalog Number
Printed in The United States of America
T-Square Graphics
Savannah, Georgia

Dedication

This book is dedicated to Lila C. Cobb, my wife of twenty- six years, who has remained calm at my side through a few bizarre encounters with friendly poltergeists. A very special thank you I give to both of my boys, Albert L. Cobb Jr. (Lee) and Jason Aaron Cobb, for their sheer bravery as well as love and support, and to my daughter, Jennifer Tara Cobb, who won "Danny's" heart with her coloring book.

Table of Contents

Albert L. Cobb Sr.

Since meeting "Danny," the seven-year-old poltergeist, our home hasn't been the same. The antique oak bed I gave my son Jason for an early Christmas gift turned out to be haunted by little "Danny." My original intention was to study this "intelligent poltergeist spirit" and report my findings in a daily journal. The journal basically wrote itself. I kept a day-to-day scorecard of each phenomenon that took place in our presence. "Danny" was only the first of many disembodied spirits that made themselves known to us.

Over the last two years we have been visited by many unknown spectral entities. I have had to enlist the services of friends, priests, and para- psychologists to help my family and me determine the nature of poltergeists and what these spirits are trying to convey to us. I have likened my home to that of Ebenezer Scrooge in Charles Dickens' classic "A Christmas Carol" and our experiences to those described in an *Outer Limits* or *Twilight Zone* episode. What began with one "spirit" has grown to include many others.

A fan of supernatural stories since I was a teenager, I have collected numerous books and magazines on the subject. I had read of families who had had poltergeist visitations, but never in my wildest dreams could I have anticipated that paranormal entities would make themselves comfortable in our home!

We don't live in an ancient, dilapidated structure one would normally find ghosts inhabiting. Our home was built in the early 1990's and is very modern. It was built on colonial farmland that was once owned by an early Georgian colonist named Noble Jones, whom the land was chartered to in the early 1730's.

We, the living, had never encountered anything in any way supernatural, and I counted myself as something of a skeptic until I learned differently on October 5, 1998. It was then I became aware of a seven-year-old poltergeist named "Danny." Most people never realize that various spirits are with us twenty-four hours a day and seven days a week. Many times my family have been awakened out of a sound sleep late at night or in the wee morning hours by scratches, footsteps, attic noises, and unexplained bumps in the night. We all have our personal spirit guides and guardian angels, but few people recognize these spirits' interventions on our behalf. Most guides and angels communicate with the living through mental telepathy. Their main function is to keep us on the proper path and guide us away from harm.

The only family that I have read about that has had as many spirits running around as we have is the Manning family in Oakham, England. In the mid - 1970's, fifteen-year-old Matthew Manning and his family experienced similar poltergeist interactions in which objects moved around their home with no possible human involvement. According to the book *The Link*, published in 1987 by Colin Smythe, Gerralds Cross, Buckinghamshire, Matthew was the poltergeist "agent" that first attracted the spirit to his family. Matthew Manning has since grown up and gained notoriety as a spiritual healer.

We still, on an almost day-to-day or week-to-week basis, experience the paranormal activity of spirits in our home. Our story has not ended, nor do I know where these experiences will lead. I just put my faith in our Lord, Jesus Christ, and as long as these spirits are comfortable with living with us in a Christian home, I have no problem with them remaining. In case such a visitation should ever happen to you, just place your fate in God's hands, and he will guide you through it. I hope this book will help people in all walks of life whether they believe in the supernatural or not.

Albert L. Cobb Sr.
Savannah, Georgia
December, 1999

Foreword

What would you do if the furniture in your house began mysteriously to rearrange itself? What if lights and electrical appliances turned themselves on and off with no apparent human intervention? What would you do if the stable, down-to-earth members of your own family began reporting phantom figures dressed in costumes of bygone eras, who spoke to them and then vanished without a trace? What would you do?

These are the questions that Al and Lila Cobb and their children had to face when the purchase of an antique bed for their son's Christmas gift triggered a ghostly presence in their home which continues to manifest itself to this day.

This book is a firsthand account of one family's incredible odyssey into the paranormal. It encompasses levitation, ghostly communication, otherworldly messages, and spectral visitations from the dead. It is the story of ghostly encounters which might have sprung from the mind of Stephen King or Peter Straub, but unlike the fictions of those distinguished authors, this story is true.

In this modern world it is easy to delude ourselves into thinking that science has discovered the answers to the most of the important questions of life. Therefore, anything inexplicable must be an hallucination or misinterpretation of some kind. Yet every new achievement by physicists, geneticists, and astronomers takes us a little bit closer to the realization that we are still far from understanding the ultimate nature of reality. In spite of incredible advances in our understanding of the brain and human behavior, psychologists still readily admit that we have no idea what the mind actually is.

Parapsychology, or psychic research, is one of the most important fields of scientific endeavor, and of all the mysteries investigated within that field, none is more intriguing, baffling, and bizarre than hauntings and poltergeists.

The existence of these ghostly phenomena is still considered controversial by many scientists, yet for those of us engaged in parapsychological studies, they are thoroughly documented and their existence is beyond dispute. Numerous scientists of world renown have admitted that the evidence for the existence of such occurrences is overwhelming in quantity, and a number of them have witnessed such things for themselves. From a researcher's point of view, I have had the good fortune to have personally witnessed poltergeist and haunting manifestations and examples of major phenomena during experimental seances.Previously, little attention was paid to reports of ghostly phenomena, and the cases that were circulated were widely considered by the educated to be the product of superstition and folklore. In earlier times, the explanation was simply witchcraft. Today the picture has changed dramatically. Accounts of hauntings and poltergeist cases are frequently described in newspapers and there are several specialty magazines that feature unexplained phenomena of all kinds, from UFO's to phantoms and angelic encounters. As a result of this growing availability of information, it would be easy for someone to acquire a bit of ephemeral fame by falsely claiming to be the victim of a haunting. In spite of the number of cases that have been invented or improved upon, there are many which are absolutely real. The prudent parapsychologist first eliminates the possibility of fraud and mis-perception, and then the study can truly begin.

Spectral phenomena can be loosely divided into two classes: Poltergeists, or pseudo-hauntings, technically known as Recurrent Spontaneous Psychokinesis (RSPK), and genuine hauntings. Poltergeist manifestations include the movement of furniture and objects, mysterious knocks and raps, showers of stones, spontaneous fires and mysterious influxes of water. Hauntings consist of very similar phenomena to that of the poltergeist, but are more sporadic and less dynamic. Hauntings also typically include unexplained sounds suggestive of human activity, such as voices, footsteps, or music. Another feature of the haunting is the appearance of the classic ghost, or apparition. Poltergeist phenomena are typically shorter in duration than hauntings, most lasting only several weeks or months, with a few cases continuing for a year or more. Hauntings, on the other hand, may last for years or decades, and occasionally centuries.

The phantoms observed in haunting cases are often connected with some past tragedy, such as a murder or suicide, as represented by local tradition. The most striking difference between these classes of phenomena, however, is their focus. Hauntings are connected to a particular location, and may be experienced by successive families over long periods of time. Poltergeist manifestations are usually dependent upon the presence of a particular person, known as the agent. Poltergeists agents are typically adolescents with psychological problems, especially repressed hostility and low tolerance for frustration. Poltergeist phenomena are generally less patterned and less intelligent than haunting. Hauntings are more "spiritoid" in nature and give the appearance of being caused by actual, independent spirits of the dead. Whether or not these apparent spirits are true entities, or merely the projections of the subject's mind, is another problem. I am inclined to combine poltergeist phenomena and hauntings into one general group, and I find it very arbitrary and difficult to sharply distinguish between them. Identical phenomena are found in both classes. Ghostly appearances, movement of objects , and sounds of all descriptions are found with both classes of phenomena. Poltergeists and hauntings represent a tremendous challenge to science. They show that there is a link between matter and mind, and they suggest the existence of forces and dimensions of our world not dreamed of in our established philosophies. To me, the prospect of exploring those dimensions and harnessing those forces for our benefit is far more exciting than merely witnessing an apparition or watching a tea cup fly across the room, and I believe this prospect is a very real one.

The nature of ghosts and poltergeists is only partially understood, but I believe that a large part of the phenomena observed originates from within the subconscious mind of an inadvertent "medium" and represents one facet of the mind temporarily acting in an apparently independent fashion. I believe also that, in certain cases, the intervention of the dead does occur.

If I were writing the foreword for a supernatural novel, I would assure the reader that the following characters are fictitious and bear no resemblance to any persons living or dead. But this is not a novel, and all the characters are real (all the living ones, that is - I can't vouch for the identities of those who claim to be dead). The experiences of the Cobb family that are related in the following pages encompass the wide variety of psychic phenomena reported by victims of hauntings and poltergeists throughout history.

Many books have been written about ghosts and paranormal phenomena. Most focus on the experiences and the author's interpretation of them. I think that the most important aspect of the Cobbs' account is the human experience itself. Above all, such occurrences are a challenge to a family's courage, determination, and curiosity in the face of seemingly inexplicable and sometimes frightening events.

Andrew Nichols, Ph.D.
Professor of Psychology, City of Gainesville College
Gainesville, Florida

Andrew Nichols, PhD.
Professor of Psychology, City College
Gainesville, Florida
Investigates our poltergeist phenomena

Savannah's Ghost and Spectres
are Locked in It's History

A long the southeastern seaboard between Hilton Head, South Carolina to the north and Jacksonville, Florida to the south lay the Savannah tropical grasslands and the city I call home, Savannah, Georgia, Her past is steeped in legend and American history made by the Indians of several thousand years ago and the English settlers who laid out the plans for the town in 1733. From the time of the revolution to the great tragedy of the Civil War, Savannah has figured prominently in all American history. She has taken part in all wars both declared and undeclared with all her man power and muscle since then.

In her two hundred and sixty four years of settlement, Savannah has seen share of ups and downs. The majority of the first influx of inhabitants were farmers, fisherman, builders and tradesman. The women and children worked at home, and the family was stronger than ever in the survival skills of the day - to - day eighteenth century activities. No one knew the great tragedies that lay directly ahead in the form of a minuscule mosquito bite and the dark clouds that would soon surround its people.

Most of the people in Savannah worked and played outdoors. The tidal creeks and low lying marshland was a perfect breeding ground for a tiny dark - colored mosquito whose Latin name is Aedes Aegypti, a carrier of a the deadly disease "Yellow Fever" called "Yellow lack" by the colonials.

From the time General Oglethorpe landed on February 12, 1733 to the landing of the first Jewish settlers on July 11, 1733, many passed away from this unknown disease caused by the bite of an infected mosquito.

In the year 1820, over 800 died from "Yellow Jack" and the disease returned and killed hundreds more in 1854 and 1876. Several thousand settlers died over the early to late nineteenth century from the three outbreaks. After being bitten by an infected mosquito the victim would run a high fever causing nausea, lightheadedness and hemorrhaging. Skin color would become as yellow as a ripe lemon. Death would soon follow. This is where "Yellow Fever" received its name.

The Colonial Cemetery is filled with the victims of the "Yellow Fever" epidemics that devastated early Georgia settlers. Many of the victims were young innocent children and many doctors who tried in vain to save them and contracted the plaque themselves.

An early American sampler that a young girl hand sketched in 1841 read,

Life is the emblem of a flower,
That buds and blossoms in an hour.
It's subject to the same decay,
For time and death sweep all away.

The people of Savannah are friendly and warm and as easy going as their ancestors of two hundred and sixty years ago. There is absolutely no other south Georgia town as rich in architecture and steeped in history.

Savannah's romantic and slow sauntering pace lends itself to tales of superstition and the occult. I have made every effort to report only genuine encounters in which local Savannahians met with the supernatural. One thing that all individuals had in common was the fact they are all just plain folk. My own run-in with the occult and paranormal universe did not take place till I was forty five years old.

We have all had some sort of inexplicable occurrence take place in our lives. Sometime we made the conscious decision not to go on plane, train or automobile which ended up in a tragedy. We simply thanked our lucky stars we were steered away for whatever reason. The truth is that we all have spirit guides which unbeknownst to most of us, telepathically guide and protect us in a safe and right direction. Most of these spirit guides are deceased family members who thrive on protecting their descendants from harm and this is a form of heaven for them.

I have not met my spirit guides but I have been advised by a psychic that two spirits walk closely with me in my daily life. Those who are gifted with "the sight" can see these spirits that walk the earth. They often communicate with them and exchange information from the other side.

Some sensitives are born with this ability to be clairaudiant by hearing the voices of the dead and unborn spirits. This can get to be a real hassle if too many of these entitles try to get on board with the mediums thoughts all at once. Occasionally, they have to mentally block off these spirits which hunger for human communication from time to time. They thrive off the life force that we the living exude. They are drawn by children and young adolescents that are in puberty since their life-force is much stronger.

In my own home, I have lately experienced the return of the spirit of my son Jason's deceased parakeet, Jacob. Jacob's cage sits empty upstairs but the little trapeze he used to perch on has been seen by us swinging to and fro. We have heard the chatter he made when he was happy and the loud screeches he made when frightened. We also heard the flapping of his wings and the sounds of his little feet scraping the wire in his cage as he flitted about. Our pet Snoodle, "Lady's" ears perked right up when she heard Jacob cry out as well.

Another bizarre occurrence happened the other night as my wife, Lila, and I lay in bed. Our Westminster grandfather clock sounded the hour. Instead of Westminster chimes, it played a strange musical box tune that sounded much to us like "Love Story." I asked Lila, "Did you hear that?" and she confirmed she had. We could never figure out how this was remotely possible. I have witnessed a dark, shadowy apparition fleeting by in our downstairs hallway. The chandeliers have been caught freely swinging with no human intervention and the sink stopper has twice flown out of the sink and landed on the floor a few years away.

For those who wish to learn more about the supernatural and paranormal in Savannah, Georgia, contact "The Searchers," c/o Beth Ronberg, P.O. Box 2054,

Savannah, Georgia 31402. I am extremely grateful to the people who have shared their poltergeist and ghost stories with me and my readers. It takes a strong person to admit he or she has seen a ghost, spirit, or other supernatural entity. As we move into the next millennium, our eyes and hearts and minds are going to be opened up to the full extent of what God intended for us to learn and experience.

Albert L. Cobb Sr.

SEARCHERS
P.O. Box 2054
Savannah, GA 31402

November 16, 1998

Mr. Al Cobb
346 Whitaker St.
Savannah, GA 31401

Dear Mr. Cobb:

Thank you for inquiring about our group "Searchers". We have enclosed a questionare about our group and would be pleased if you could take some time to fill it out and return it to us.

"Searchers" has been in existence since 1996 and has been involved in various types of research and exploration of supernatural and paranormal occurences in and around Savannah. We are not limited to investigating local phenomena, although there is an abundance of research to be done here alone. Our group members come from all walks of life and all have a genuine interest in the historical as well as the paranormal facts regarding a haunting. Our group normally meets at least twice a month, and we try to schedule a site visit once a month. There are times when a site is visited many times over, in order to fully investigate the phenomena there.

All of our group members participate in business meetings as well as site visits. We are flexible as far as other commitments, but strongly encourage an active participation in the group. If you feel that you are willing to make such a commitment to our group, please return the enclosed forms and we will be in contact with you very shortly.

Thank you for your interest in "Searchers". We hope to hear back from you soon!

Happy Haunting!

Sincerely,

Beth Ronberg
Charter Member - Searchers

Biography of
Albert L. Cobb, Sr.

I was born November 6, 1953 in Tulsa, Oklahoma, and, after graduating from Savannah Christian School here in Savannah in 1972, I began my first job a year later in the retail jewelry business at Desbouillions Jewelers. A year after that, on July 3, 1974, I married my high school sweetheart and fellow classmate Lila C. Cobb. We have three children. Our daughter, Jennifer Tara Cobb, was born in 1979 and was followed in 1984 by our twin sons, Albert L. Cobb Jr., whom we call Lee, and Jason Aaron Cobb. After I left the jewelry business, I opened my own antique shop and appraisal service in 1981.

This is the first book I have ever written. I still appraise and sell antiques daily. I am called on by my customers and by insurance companies who need appraisals for many different reasons. I appraise coins, stamps, jewelry, paintings, art pottery, silver, gold, and all other collections of all catagories including modern limited editions and autographs. I am a member of the American Art Pottery Association, and my firm is listed on Dunn and Bradstreet. My hobbies include fishing, stamp collecting, coin collecting, metal detecting, and collecting television shows and movies in VHS format.

Chapter One

Our True Experiences with Poltergeists in Savannah

I am a believer in the world of the eternal spirit, a world that exists just on the fringe of the three dimensional plane of our own. It is inhabited by yet unborn spirits coupled with the spirits of those who led an earthly life. Many haven't moved on into the Creator's white light we know as heaven. This "Heaven" is referred to by spiritualists as "Summerland."

My wife, Lila, my daughter, Jennifer, and my fraternal twin sons, Albert Jr. (who we call Lee) and Jason Cobb live in a typical one story home in Savannah, Georgia. Both Lila and I are graduates of Savannah Christian School, Class of 1972. We were high school sweethearts and both come from a Southern Baptist background. Lila was the salutatorian of our class and gave the salutatory address at our commencement exercises.

I am an antiques and collectibles dealer with my own gallery since 1981. I have also been an appraiser of art and antiques since 1975. Nothing out of the ordinary, especially pertaining to the supernatural, had taken place in our lives before moving into our home in the Isle of Hope area. As a hobby, I collect comedy, science-fiction, horror, and blockbuster classic movies in VHS home library format. My daughter, Jennifer, had recently moved away but would still drop in from time to time, and we kept her abreast of what was taking place in the house during her absence.

Lila, the boys, and I attended the preview of an upcoming auction taking place the following day at The Savannah Galleries Auction House on Indian Street. Jason had been longing for an antique bed for sometime, and he spied an interesting golden oak bed C.1890 sitting off in the corner of the gallery. It seemed to be in excellent condition with simple applied molding and carving on the head and footboard. Lila and I decided to leave an absentee bid on it for Jason as a Christmas gift. When I returned to the gallery the next day the auctioneer, Jim Donnelly, told me we had bought the bed with our bid of $125.00. I had it loaded into my Volvo and parked outside my shop when Lila came by in her Windstar and took the bed home to surprise Jason. How thrilled Jason would be! She soon had the bed settled in Jason's room. It seemed to add a warm glow to the room. Jason beamed from ear to ear with excitement. By that afternoon as I returned from my shop, I saw how pleased Jason was with his bed, and I was glad we made the purchase.

Jason's first night sleeping in the bed was comfortable enough even though he was experiencing an odd breath of cold air on his neck and an eerie sensation that he was being watched. He attributed the air on his neck to the air vent in the ceiling and the feeling of being watched to something he had eaten. That feeling of queasiness that Jason experienced was like the sudden drop of an elevator, the same motion sickness he felt when riding around in a car traveling for long distances or a rough boat ride that caused an uneasiness within his stomach. This is the way he felt constantly when he was watched. Jason felt all these emotions centering around the bed when he either sat or slept on it.

Jason began to get a strong sensation of feeling hot and feverish and sick to his stomach. Now, for the first time, he felt the presence of another entity in the room with him. This odd feeling was confirmed on the third night when he felt one side of his bed press downward as a cool breath blew on the back of his neck as if someone were lying beside him. The feeling of eyes watching him was powerful. He tossed and turned in the bed and vividly remembered his pillows falling off the bed in the middle of the night, but he was too tired to retrieve them. Mysteriously, the next morning they were back in place on his bed!

Jason continued to experience these phenomenon without our knowledge for the next two weeks until on Sunday morning, October 5, 1998, he confided to Lila what had been going on in his room since the bed's arrival. He showed Lila that the picture of her deceased parents, Felton and Ruth Crosby, which he kept on a wicker lamp table on the side of his bed was constantly found lying face down. He would set the picture frame straight and do no more than turn around and the photo would be face down again.

Lila told Jason that there had to be a logical reason for the picture frame to fall repeatedly over on its face. Maybe the wicker lamp table was off balance or the picture frame support was too weak to keep the picture upright. Lila suggested that they place the photograph in its proper upright position and then walk out of the room and shut the door behind them. Both Jason and Lila were both surprised when they came back moments later and the photograph was down on its face again. "Let's try it again," Lila said as she and Jason reset the picture and walked out a second time, shutting the door behind them. On their re-entry into the room, the photograph was again on its face only this time it had crossed the room to another table! "Impossible," Lila exclaimed as she and Jason backed out of the room and brought me back to the room to show me what had taken place. As Lila explained the situation, my immediate thoughts were that Jason's brother, Lee, was hiding in the room and playing a joke. This wasn't the case as Lee was off on his bicycle and had been away from the house, so I had to rule out teen trickery. My second thought was that Lila and Jason were trying to play a prank on me, but they both were deadly serious.

Lila suggested that we upright the photos again and all walk out of the room together and close the door behind us. This is exactly what we did and no one had access to the room, since we stayed together outside the door for ten minutes. By this time Lee had arrived and waited with us. While we waited, we thought we heard small scraping sounds coming from behind the closed door.

After a few more moments, Lila and I entered first, followed by Jason and Lee. As we opened the door, I was suddenly transported from a quiet Sunday morning in a typical southern household to a setting reminiscent of *The Twilight*

Zone, *Poltergeist*, or Charles Dickens' "A Christmas Carol." The pictures were down on their faces and moved around again. Repeating the experiment, we found the photograph upright, but the picture frame's glass shattered as if hit directly in the center with a blunt object. We did not know what to think and found ourselves wondering how this could be real. We walked out and shut the door behind us again. We now played a waiting game to see what would happen next.

At 11:40 A.M. we opened the door and this time other items had been moved in Jason's room and placed in the center of his bed. A six-inch shell figural, a T-Rex, and a medium-sized conch shell were on the bed. In addition, two Beanie Babies that had been on his dresser were now sitting in the middle of an old, oak swivel chair beside his bed. Nothing ever moved or levitated in front of us, but every time that door would close, things changed position in the room.

After taking a thirty-minute break with the door closed, we came back to the room to find the two Beanie Babies, a tiger, and a zebra lying on the bed side by side. Clearly visible, were children's fingerprints on their necks as if, together, the toys had been picked up by some unknown force and carried from the seat of the oak, swivel chair to the bed.

I was beginning to realize that we may have been dealing with an intelligent male child spirit, and I did not want the opportunity for communication to pass. I could feel the hairs on my arms and the back of my neck begin to stand on end, and a strange coolness enveloped the room. I know that "our little man" had taken the first step to let us know that he existed and apparently wished to communicate with us.

Having absolutely no prior knowledge about how to begin such an endeavor, I simply said the first thing that popped into my head: "Casper, is that you?" "Are you a little, six-year-old boy who has been playing with my son's toys?"

The room remained quiet, but the coolness was still prevalent in the room. I called out to "Casper" again. No answer came forth, but I noticed that a brightly colored toucan bird bank had been moved from a high corner shelf down to the floor near Jason's closet door. I felt a little embarrassed to be speaking out loud to thin air, but I really felt that something was indeed with us in the room. I asked myself, "Where do we take it from here?"

Lila , the boys, and I discussed the possibilities and decided to clean the room and straighten it up, putting the toys back in the closet and making the bed. We all walked out and shut Jason's door behind us. As we stood in the dining room and hallway just outside the door, there was definite movement inside the room. We could hear the closet door sliding open and the hangers making a high-pitched clinking sound as they bounced off each other. There was a bumping sound as if shoes were being tossed off the wall in the back of the closet. Lila and I closely monitored Jason and Lee as they stood beside us for about five minutes until the sounds ceased. Finally, I could stand it no longer, and I knocked on the door. As I slowly turned the doorknob, I announced we were entering the room.

All four of us were astounded. Not only were the Beanie Babies back on the bed, but the conch shell, a carved African elephant, and a purple "Shakesbear" teddy bear greeted us in the center of Jason's bed. I told everyone that I had a strong feeling that "our little boy" was having a wonderful time playing impish pranks on us. Our hearts were beating a mile a minute from the exhilaration we all felt from our meager attempts to communicate with this young spirit. Through a kind of sixth sense, Jason could feel the moment he entered the room where the young spirit was and what it was up to. Lila and I could only stand by and try to make some adult sense out of all this. The room was put back in order for another attempt to communicate. This time, I left out a single Nabisco Cameo cream sandwich cookie on a paper plate in the center of the bed. I called out to our little visitor that he was welcome to help himself to the little snack. We turned out the lights, shut the door, and left the room for fifteen minutes.

It was 1:30 A.M. and time to check on our little visitor. We were so involved in our project that we did not think about going to bed. Once again, we knocked on the door and slowly turned the doorknob. In the middle of the paper plate lay the cookie pulled apart with one side icing and one side cookie. On the icing side we could barely see a slight fingernail impression of a child! Not just four, but eleven of Jason's toys were removed from the closet and were placed surrounding the cookie plate. The photo of Lila's mother and father lay beside the cookie plate as well. More evidence was found at the head of the bed on Jason's pillow. The distinct impression of a child's head was on the pillows. I called out again for the little boy to communicate with us again. This time I told him I was leaving out a sheet of paper and a pen for him to write his name and age on it. I left them on a small trunk at the foot of the bed, walked out of the room, and shut the door behind me. When I returned fifteen minutes later, the pen had been moved and written on the surface of the paper in the stick-figure style of a child was "Danny 7."

First Contact
Sunday, October 5, 1998 at 1:14 p.m.

**1890's era engraving of what "Danny" looks like
when he materializes in our house.**

This was the first breakthrough, one that we had stayed up all night to achieve. Now we had a name and an age for the spirit that had made himself known to us. I had at least a hundred questions for our guest, but it had been like pulling teeth just to get his name and age. He never gave us a clue about his last name, and it was a long time before we were able to learn his origin.

I was elated that at last we had some physical evidence that our child spirit "Danny" was real. "Hi, Danny," I said. "I'm going to leave out a new box of colored pencils and more sheets of paper for you to write on!" I asked "Danny" to tell us what connection he had with the antique bed. Before the bed's arrival, we had never had a supernatural act take place in our home, at least not that we knew of, although I was aware of documented, eyewitness accounts and case histories of haunted furniture becoming animated and affecting people's lives.

I pulled out a small stack of white, letter-sized typing paper and a box of Crayola colored pencils and left them on the trunk at the foot of Jason's bed. This is the area where "Danny" had written to us before. We shut the door and waited patiently.

It was nearing two in the morning, but we could not sleep. I held the signature of this spirit and studied it in disbelief that we were contacting an entity from the other side; somehow it didn't seem real. "Danny's" handwriting wasn't that different from a typical seven-year old's. The straight, top-to-bottom lines and teepee-style "A's" and "N's" are common characteristics of a young child's handwriting. This sort of writing occurs when children are learning to hold a pencil for the first time. Their small hands have difficulty grasping writing implements, so they form their letters in a top- to-bottom motion that resembles unsteady, stick-like writing.

Fifteen more minutes had passed. It was time to go downstairs to see if "Danny" had left a written answer to our second question. Lila chose to be the first to gently rap on the door. She slowly turned the knob to Jason's room, and we crowded in close behind her and entered the room. Suddenly, Lila let out a gasp! "AL, AL, look! Look! How did my graduation picture get from in the living room to here?" Lila's portrait was on the floor in front of the trunk at the foot of Jason's bed. "Danny" must have somehow left Jason's room and taken the framed photograph from the Cuban mahogany empire table in the corner of our living room!

The old oak bed was covered with toys from one end to the other. "Danny" really put on a show to impress us that he could move objects in our plane. Crazy and oddball items were pulled from the bottom of the closet, including Lila's dad's electric foot massager and a tall, realistic, rubber doll, a Siamese dancer, a collector's item. There was a can of fish food on the floor pulled down from the side of the aquarium. Scattered around the bed were fifteen different toys that "Danny" hadn't touched before—a china figurine of a baby panda, and other items, like wooden elephant carvings and new Beanie Babies, things were getting stranger by the moment.

I was most impressed by "Danny's" second note and its contents. Using a light, lead pencil "Danny" wrote, "MOM-SICK IN BED, DIED 1899, LOVE TOYS!" He had crossed out an extra "O" he had written in the word "LOVE" and x'ed over his error before he wrote the final "E." Now, we had some kind of handle on this bizarre situation. We knew that we were dealing with a seven-year old child male spirit, who loved toys.

Why, then, did he choose the room of our fourteen-year old to make contact in? Was he drawn to Jason's aura or life force? What caused "Danny" to suddenly wake up from his one hundred-year-old sleep? I knew I had a lot to learn about the world of the paranormal. I spoke out loud to "Danny" that we all needed our rest now and that we couldn't stay up and play with him all night! I knew if we slept at all we would have to get back up in two hours. Our heads were numb as we cleaned Jason's room up after each time Danny "played."

We chose to restore the room to its original condition, the way it was before "Danny" had manifested himself, and go to bed. This was the ninth time we left the room and shut the door behind us. Lila and I tried to settle into our bed, but we never really went to sleep. Our hearts were still beating wildly with the excitement of communicating with "Danny." Jason was sleeping in his brother Lee's room. We were advised by a local Catholic priest that it would be better if he did not sleep on the bed. I had spread holy water throughout the bedroom and surrounding rooms in the house. You can't be too sure if you're dealing with a benign spirit or not.

Not five minutes passed from when our heads hit our pillows when Lila and I heard Jason and Lee calling out to us to come back to Jason's room. The door was still closed but the walls shook with loud pounding sounds like there was a fight going on in the room. There was a loud knocking sound in the closet that echoed down the hallway like a bass drum. Bumping noises and the distinct sound of a light bulb popping caused me to throw open the door and see what the chaos was all about. The scene I witnessed in the room made my heart jump up into my throat. Everywhere I looked, things were tossed about!

The room looked as though a bomb had exploded at ground point zero. The pole lamp in the corner was flat on the floor as if it had been stomped on, and the bulb that we heard explode in the hallway was shattered. The old, oak swivel office chair was pushed down on its side. A small, terra-cotta statue of a boy's head from a wall pocket had its camphor sprig contents spread out all around the bed and the floor. The colored pencils, papers, and markers that we left out for "Danny" were tossed from one end of the room to the other. "Danny" had written "MEAN MAN!" in a dark marker with a bright orange glow. This was the start of what was to be a series of short notes and observations that Danny would continue to write to each family member for over a year. Jason could sense the father of "Danny" had gotten wind that his son was visiting us and tried to draw "Danny" back to the other side, but "Danny" refused to go. "Danny" communicated to Jason that he never liked his father and referred to him as the "MEAN MAN."

To put it mildly, it was difficult for the boys to get up on Monday and get to their classes at the Savannah Arts Academy. With about thirty minutes sleep, I dragged myself into my antiques shop and called Lila back at the house to make sure she was okay. Generally, she takes Mondays off, but she is always very active with yard work and inside and outside activities. Lila kept the door to Jason's room open all day hoping "Danny" wouldn't try any shenanigans while she was home alone. She felt nervous and fidgety and our little female dog "Lady" stayed close by Lila's heels all day. Nonetheless, Lila remained vigilant, listening for any strange sounds or movements around her, but the house remained silent.

At 3:20 in the afternoon the boy's school bus dropped them off on the corner. They were both anxious to learn if anything had happened in the house in their absence. Jason asked Lila if "Danny" had written any more messages and she told him no. Lee was quick to add that momma had not closed the door and then proceeded to shut it. Lila asked Jason to water the flowers on the front porch, so Jason dropped his book bag and turned and walked out the front door. Still curious as to why "Danny" didn't write anything, Jason strolled over to his bedroom windows and peeked into his darkened room. As he shielded his eyes, adjusting them to the afternoon sun that was streaming in under the porch's roof, he suddenly caught a quick movement in the center of his bed. There laid one of the set of leather bound editions of Sir Walter Scott's "Waverly" novels that he had bought from the same auction house that the bed came from! This volume was standing open and the pages were flipping as if an invisible speed reader were searching each chapter.

Jason ran back into the house and told his mother and brother what he had just witnessed on the porch. Jason's sixth sense was buzzing, and he told them that "Danny" was still playing in the room and they could all hear him moving things about. The three of them opened the door and found at the foot of Jason's bed the rest of the "Waverly" novels stacked on top of each other, but the one on top was opened and turned to page three hundred and ninety-four. There were a couple of paragraphs in chapter thirty-six pertaining to a child and his toys. To paraphrase, it said "But love made him a child. He throws down and treads on these costly toys, with the same vehemence would he dash to pieces this frailest toy of all, of which he used to rave so fondly. But that taste also will be forgotten when its object is no more." We believe that "Danny" was again trying to communicate with us by using the paragraphs in these books, but only an English scholar could possibly make sense of what "Danny" was trying to tell us.

Lila and the boys then closed the door and she took them to the doctor's for their yearly physical. Before they walked out the door Lila said, "Come on, boys. Let's let "Danny" get some rest. He's tired." After dinner, Lila opened the door to Jason's room and left a note asking "Danny" why he had broken the glass in her parents' photograph the previous day. Thirty minutes later she returned to find an apology written in a light blue-colored pencil saying, "SORRY LILA."

Danny's second contact letter.

Lila's graduation portrait

At 7:30 p.m. "Danny" started shifting pictures around the room again. The side-table pictures were laid on the pillows at the head of the bed. We kept the door shut but were continuing to monitor everything he did. Playtime had arrived! In the next hour and a half, "Danny" pulled most of the toys out of Jason's closet so that during the evening during our observation checks we left a note to "Danny" asking him if we could help him find the light. The priest who gave us the holy water had also advised us to keep asking if we could help him find the light, but in his usual straightforward way "Danny" wrote back to us: "WANT TO STAY WITH BED," "SAW MOM." We knew that he was aware that he and his mother are dead, but being a free spirit "Danny" seemed to view my family as the neighbors just across the street. His momma has told him to stay in his own yard but as soon as she turns her back he comes over to our dimensional plane to play.

"Danny" had always seemed very warm towards Lila. I wondered why he spent so much time looking and reviewing her deceased parents' photographs. He included moving the photographs around in almost every "play time" episode since his arrival in our home. He traveled to the other side of the "vail" to speak with them on Lila's behalf without her knowledge. We know that without a shadow of doubt because "Danny" is multi-dimensional and had already gone outside the confines of Jason's room and retrieved Lila's graduation picture and had written a personal note of apology for breaking the glass in the photograph of her mom and dad. Lila placed a small plastic duck inside an airplane "Happy Meal" toy out for him, and he wrote back to her: "Thank you for the toy Lila." This time "Danny" picked out Lila's mother's mixing bowl from the top shelf in our kitchen and carried it back to Jason's room. Out of a country mixing bowl collection numbering over thirty bowls, "Danny" picked the right one! Next, "Danny" chose an Andre Sadek yellow songbird figurine that Lila had inherited from her mother from the collection of birds that we keep in a corner curio cabinet. Not only was this bird her mother's favorite, but it was the first bird that started her collection. Something that wasn't her mother's but probably reminded him of her mother was an angel that stands about eleven inches tall and is made of terra-cotta that we keep on our kitchen counter. This four-pound religious figure also found its way to the top of the trunk at the foot of Jason's bed.

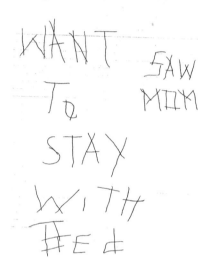

**Monday October 6, 1988
at 7:40 p.m.
"Danny" was playing with his toys all day. He left this message concerning his intentions to stay and play with his mom's permission, of course.**

For a grand finale, "Danny" wrote Lila this note: "Your Mom's Bowl Lila", and he had drawn an arrow pointing to the bowl. In addition, he wrote her that he talked to them: "Saw Them, They Miss and Love You, Very Happy!" The amount of kinetic energy that "Danny" exhausted to create such a sweet little monument and to write the notes could not be measured. He added "Tired, Sleeptime." When I wrote him a second time to ask him his last name, he refused to tell me, perhaps because he was too cautious or perhaps because he was just too tired. "Secret AL," he wrote. I think his refusal to give us more information stemmed from his fear that we would try to investigate his past, and he is right. Spirits are forewarned by God and angels not to divulge too many secrets to mortals, as we will soon learn what the Father wishes us to know in His own good time.

I walked back to our bedroom, and just as I was nearing my side of the bed, I tripped over Lila's makeup bag. "Danny" strikes again! Lila always keeps her bag in the second drawer of the bathroom cabinet, yet here it was under my bed. We seemed to have a strange "child spirit" running amok throughout our house and there was nothing we could do about it. It was like having a wild, seven-year-old child living with us and we couldn't really control him. He had been into every room in the house and his curiosity was unceasing.

I was amazed at "Danny's" ability to bring back information from the other side, so I dreamed up a mission for him to go on for me. My father, Robert A. Cobb, had passed away on November 18, 1984. He was a heavy smoker most of his life and suffered and died from lung cancer. I found an old 8x10 unframed photograph of my dad taken in 1943. He was dressed in his first class, Navy radioman dress blues. I carried the photograph back to Jason's room and placed it with a note on the foot of the bed. I asked "Danny" to find him and ask how he was doing and whether he was happy? I left the room shutting the door behind me. For a few moments, I listened at the door, and then I walked away.

This is a 1943 photograph of my dad, Robert A. Cobb. He was a First Class Radioman in the U.S. Navy at the time photo was taken by Tooley Myron Studios, 119 E. Broughton Street, Savannah, Georgia.

Fifteen minutes later, "Danny" penned a message on the trunk at the foot of the bed: "Sorry Al, No Connect Yet, Tired." Verbally, I told him to get some rest and try again later when he felt up to it and to let me know what he found out.

Jason was home sick from school the next morning, and Lee had gone on to catch the school bus. I instructed Jason as to what I was doing and to call me at my office the moment that "Danny" left another message.

Within an hour after my arrival at the office, Jason called me and, judging by the sound of the quivering in his voice, I could tell he was very nervous and frightened. He was calling me from the upstairs phone in our bonus room to say that he had heard a lot of things bumping and moving downstairs and the sound of drawers being opened. He wanted to know whether he should go to investigate. I tried to calm his fears, telling him that I was sure it was only "Danny" and not to be afraid. I told him to check it out and that I would stay on the line.

In a few moments that seemed like hours he returned to the phone and gave me his scouting report. "'Danny' has been in your highboy, Dad," he said. "He wrote a note like mom's with an arrow pointing to the pictures of Grandma Cobb and Aunt Kathy and Robin and you." "There's more," he continued. "'Danny' chose pictures of you and your sisters that were taken at the age of seven." "The picture of Great Grandma Cobb and Grandma Cobb was taken out in San Francisco in the same year as your dad's Navy photograph in 1943." I almost dropped the phone receiver in astonishment. "Danny" filtered through a huge manila envelope filled with hundreds of photos of family members and he chose the right children, each at the tender age of seven years. I couldn't wait to hear what Jason was about to tell me next. The note read, "Saw Him AL , He (Nows), Loves."

I lost it. I felt a tremendous swell in my throat and chest and I cried. It was like a tiny bit of grief that I still held within me had suddenly resurfaced and filled me with deep emotion. I called my sisters and immediately told them what had happened and they, too, were highly emotional over "Danny's" keen insight for a seven-year-old child.

My daughter came over to visit and brought a Disney coloring book and a new box of crayons for "Danny." We had kept her up-to-date on the child spirit and she had a good feeling that "Danny" would use the coloring books. In fact, she was right on target. "Danny" opened the book and colored when we set the book out the next day. His work was very good for a child his age. He stayed within the lines and both Mickey and Minnie mouse were colored in black, and he used different bright colors for their clothes. It seems from this little experiment that he sees in color as we do. Every time we cleared off the bed, "Danny" dragged the Beanie Babies back out to play with them again. We left out the coloring book for him and he colored in several pages and signed his name.

Up to this time only the five members of my family in Savannah knew about the poltergeist in our home. I felt it necessary to invite a local Savannah jeweler friend of mine over to see if "Danny" would respond to him. Before I left that morning for work, I told "Danny" that we may have a visitor come over to see him at the house that evening. I also needed some kind of confirmation from someone outside the family. I had known Bryan Hoffhaus since 1973 when we both worked at Desboullion's Jewelers in Savannah, Georgia.

We had the coffee perking when Bryan arrived at 7:30 that evening. We walked back to Jason's room and I told "Danny" that Bryan had come over to see him. Next, I asked if he would please make himself known by communicating in writing or moving an object in the room. Bryan said hello and introduced himself. Then, we walked out the door and shut it behind us. We sat at the kitchen table and talked for the first fifteen minutes, then walked back to Jason's door. I turned the door knob and looked in, but this time everything remained the same. We returned to the kitchen and I began to wonder if "Danny" would make an appearance. Another fifteen minutes elapsed and we checked the room again but no cigar! I was about to get more than a little red-faced if "Danny" chose not to show up. In the back of my mind, I was reminded of the man who was auditioning his live animal act on *The Ed Sullivan Show* and couldn't get the star to perform in front of a live audience.

Forty-five minutes had now passed, and we all sat upstairs in the bonus room. I felt "Danny" needed a little more wagon room, so we chose to wait upstairs and had a fudge sickle. This time "Danny" proved me right. When we opened the door the third time, we observed that a can of fish salt had been moved from the side of the aquarium, two stuffed animals, and three Beanie Babies were on the bed. On a sheet of paper "Danny" had written, "TIRED." Bryan was impressed but nothing had moved in front of him so he could only sign off on the sheet that we had activity but no visual sightings. "Danny" had never really moved anything in front of us either, but we knew he would accomplish the mission if we shut the door. Within minutes of Bryan leaving the house, "Danny" moved a stuffed elephant from Jason's drawer to the bed and he joined them with the big purple "Shakesbear" bear and a medium-sized conch shell. "Danny's" plan was to keep the bed so full of toys that Jason would not have room to lie down. All activity ceased the rest of the night as "Danny" rested.

Danny sternly warns Jason "No one sleep in bed."

The next morning, Lila checked the room first thing when she was getting ready for work at 6:30 a.m. and everything was normal. Fifteen minutes later she looked one last time before walking out the door. The closet was wide open and "Danny" had toys strewn everywhere and a cheap pair of sunglasses that Lila had tried on the night before was lying on the bed. A note Lila wrote to "Danny" thanking him for getting in touch with her was answered, "Welcome!"

"Danny" had shown us that he was prone to like all the things that any seven-year-old child liked, so I brought down a box of red, green, blue and yellow building blocks from the upstairs bonus room. I sat them next to the closet door on the floor by Jason's bed and spoke to "Danny" to "go to it!" I walked out and shut the door once again. Both Lee and Jason were listening to the sounds of the blocks bouncing on the floor and hitting against each other. They sat just outside the hallway in the living room and heard the sounds as "Danny" played by himself in the room. We walked in and saw that he had built a wooden "gateway" sculpture with the blocks! I grabbed my digital camera and photographed the strange work of art. Was he showing us a gateway to the other side? I have talked to him and written several notes to him to tell us about God, Heaven, and Angels, but he always wrote back "Can't Tell AL, Secret!"

Danny was like having an unseen stranger listening to every private conversation you are having and critiquing its content in notes left on tables around the house. Case in point, Lee had talked back and raised his voice to Lila while I was at work and later that same afternoon a note appeared in "Danny's" writing saying, "Lee Bad to Mom - Nice!"

The little guy had to have heard Jason, Lila, and me discussing whether or not Jason should attempt to go to sleep in the bed that night because a note soon came saying, "No One Sleep in Bed!" Jason was getting a little miffed at this seven-year-old child spirit taking over his room which indeed "Danny" had. There may have been a touch of jealousy from the attention we had given to the spirit child, but we only wished to learn more about him, where he was from and why he chose to reveal himself to us. When we found out he was a good spirit and not an evil one, Jason thought it would be a good time to push one of "Danny's" buttons by pretending to feel faint and fall back on "Danny's" bed. He simply fell backwards and put his arms up over his head and sighed in a way that would tick "Danny" off.

Lila and I both told Jason to get up off the bed, but he stayed for a few more minutes just rubbing it in just a little deeper. Lila and I both warned Jason that there may be consequences for teasing "Danny." We walked out and Jason finally rose from the bed and followed close behind us. Suddenly, he decided to go back and retrieve some clothes from the floor in his closet when "Danny" couldn't take it anymore, and so he retaliated.

Just fifteen feet behind where Lila and I were standing we heard a loud crash that sounded like a shotgun blast! We raced into Jason's room and saw the terra cotta wall pocket that had hung over Jason's bed smashed to pieces at the foot of Jason's closet! "He threw it at me!" Jason exclaimed. Visibly shaken and upset to the point of tears, Jason explained he had just bent over to pick up his clothes when he heard a sound from the wall directly behind him. His keen hearing picked up a bumping and scratching sound as the terra cotta wall pocket left the wall and rocketed towards his head! He caught the movement out of the corner of his eye just a fraction of a second before it collided with the closet door, narrowly missing his head.

Lila ran over and put her arms around her still visibly-shaken son. "Don't you hurt my son!" she screamed out as she consoled Jason. Lee and I stood closely nearby, and I became very angry at "Danny" as well. "Why, Danny!" "Jason is your friend, not your enemy!" I shouted. "You apologize to Jason and tell us why you did that right now!"

There was no response. The room was quiet and we left the door open. There was a deep scratch and dent left on the left side of the closet door. Lee and I began picking up the debris of the wall pocket that lay in about a hundred and fifty pieces on the carpet. I began to understand the reasons "Danny" had for throwing the wall pocket at Jason. I knew the answer: Jason teased him about his bed. This was "Danny's" way of making Jason back off. The bed was the last thing "Danny" had an earthly tie to since he died in the bed in 1899. He had come back to visit his former possession. After an hour and a half there was still no response from "Danny" so Lila and I decided to sell the bed. I couldn't take a chance that "Danny" might start throwing knives next, so the boys and I began to disassemble the bed and load it into the back of Lila's red Windstar van parked in the driveway.

The following morning I was having breakfast at "The Delivery Room Cafe" after dropping Jason and Lee off at The Savannah Arts Academy when the waitress signaled me over to the counter and told me I had a phone call. Lila had called me from work and told me she was having a very strange feeling of remorse over how we were handling the situation with "Danny." I, too, was feeling a pang of remorse for not giving the spirit boy another chance after only one mistake. We both talked a few more minutes and decided to give "Danny" a second chance.

Lila and I had traded autos and for a change I was driving her Windstar with the bed. I returned home and unloaded the bed into our garage. I put a white sheet over it and leaned it against the wall leading to our kitchen. There was no way I could have anticipated "Danny's" reaction to "his relocation," but Jason and Lee were soon to find out when they came home from school that afternoon.

When the boys came in the front door, Lee was in the lead and they both headed back to their rooms to drop off their book bags. Lee walked by Jason's open door and took a quick look in before proceeding to his room. Everything was okay; there was just a blank area where "Danny's" bed had been. Seconds behind him, Jason walked by, and then all hell broke loose in the room! The pole lamp in the rooms corner came crashing down to the floor as the boys stood by and watched in horror. The bird cage fell over and "Jacob," Jason's little blue and white parakeet, was screaming bloody murder! The curtains were pulled off their rods and colored pencils and markers were strewn over the floor as well. Jason's clothes were yanked off their hangers and tossed like yesterday's old newspaper in a heap on the floor.

The boys ran to the kitchen phone and called to tell me that "Danny" was throwing a major tantrum and that I should come right home! I told them to get out of the house, and I would be home as soon as possible.

I set a new speed record, from downtown to the Isle of Hope in less than fifteen minutes. Jason and Lee were waiting outside for me as I pulled up into the driveway. I entered the house and saw what "Danny" had done and came back through the garage, grabbed the bed, and loaded it into my Volvo. When Jason and Lee saw the bed under the sheets in the garage, they both complained, "Dad, you didn't tell us that you brought the bed back!"

I told them we had talked on the phone at breakfast, and mom and I had decided to give "Danny" the benefit of the doubt and a second chance. I could have sworn that with the bed taken apart that "Danny's" powers would be nullified, but I got a rude awakening. We drove downtown and consigned the bed for auction with the Kramer/Sadler Gallery on McDonough Street. I thought that putting the bed out-of-sight and out-of-mind would be the best course of action, and the boys and I breathed a sigh of relief that the bed was out of our house.

The following Monday night on October 13, 1998, the bed sold to a dealer and his wife for $66.00. I wanted the new owners of the bed to know its history with our family since we had owned it for the past month. I told them about "Danny" and they seemed to take it all in stride and actually seemed elated that the bed came with a little boy spirit! The wife told me they would fix up a spare bedroom that they had for him, complete with the toys he loved to play with. I didn't feel so bad about giving "Danny" up, but I found out a very short time later they were offered $500.00 for the bed and sold it.

What made the bed so valuable in such a short period of time was a newspaper article that was written by Jane Fishman on October 16, 1998, in *The Savannah Morning News* entitled "Boy Ghost in My Bed: 'Danny's' Story--Believe it or Not!"

Jane had dropped by my office and interviewed me and then came by our house two days later and interviewed Lila and the boys. On that Friday morning when the newspaper hit the Savannah streets people began to talk about our poltergeist and to call me with many stories about poltergeists in their own homes. Jane had come by and interviewed us with more than a little apprehension. Once we showed her the "before" and "after" photos we had taken of the poltergeist's destructive capabilities and once she had heard each of our personal stories, I believe we had her full attention. I didn't get a single prank phone call. I did, however, get calls from friends and acquaintances who asked if the story was, indeed, true and when I confirmed for them that everything I had spoken of had happened just as I had described it, they began to tell me of their own paranormal experiences. I kept my journal up-to-date in triplicate, so I could pass on our experiences to those who are interested in the supernatural.

Ten days had passed since we had "given up the ghost." The bed was in a shop in Pembroke, Ga., and we were getting back to our normal lives. On Sunday morning October 18, 1998, I was preparing one of my sumptuous egg and bacon breakfasts with cheddar cheese grits and hot biscuits when Lila and Jason called me back to his bedroom again. Jason had left his door to his room open, but for some reason when he had returned from taking a shower in the bathroom, his door was shut and both he and Lee heard something moving around inside. The sound had stopped as we turned the door knob and walked in. At the foot of Jason's bed lay a stack of notebook paper that Jason told us was on his dresser when he went to take a shower. On the top sheet were written two words with a bright orange marker: "'Danny' Sorry." In the center of the bed was the little shell covered dinosaur that "Danny" moved around and played with.

Later, a stuffed Easter Bunny was found in a basket in front of Lila as she was doing the laundry, the same rabbit that she had put away in a closet and planned to give to "Danny" before his tantrums made us say "so long!" "Danny" had returned to visit us. Even without the bed, he was making himself right at home as if nothing had ever happened. I wrote down two questions for him that afternoon: "What does Danny Want" and "Why did you not stay with your bed?"

At 9:15 that evening we came downstairs from the bonus room for some coffee. Jason's door had again been left open, but from the kitchen we all heard his door shut as the door knob made a tiny "Click!" We opened the door and, sitting on the top of the trunk at the foot of Jason's bed, was the tall, standing angel figurine that "Danny" had earlier moved from the kitchen. Beneath the angel's feet "Danny" left us another communiqué: "Danny Go Up, By, By!" and "Mean Lady Sold Me!" I prayed that the good Lord would give him a safe passage to heaven and that Jesus Christ would be at the door to greet him. He actually did not mean he was ready to go just yet and would continue to write us messages. He is over one hundred years old, but still thinks and acts as a seven-year-old would. Time has no bearing on this little free spirit known to us as "Danny."

Because I thought we had a valid connection with the supernatural and because I wanted to hear from others who live in the coastal empire who may have had similar experiences, I contacted WTOC TV. We couldn't be the only ones who

Danny's story:
Believe it or not

Jason Cobb always wanted an antique bed. So for an early Christmas present, he and his dad, Al, went to the Tuesday night auction at Savannah Auction on Indian Street, where Jason made his pick — a late 1800s, honey-oak single bed with a carved headrest and some nice fancy molding at the feet.

Jane Fishman

But the night was late, so Al, who owns Cobb's Galleries on Whitaker Street, submitted a bid and the two went home. The next day, after finding out he was the high bidder, Al drove to the downtown Savannah auction house, picked up the bed and assembled the antique in Jason's bedroom in their Isle of Hope home.

So far, so good.

Three nights later, Jason, 14, wasn't so sure. He told his parents he felt as if someone had planted elbows on his pillow and was watching him and breathing cold air down the back of his neck. He felt sick.

The next night he noticed the photo of his deceased grandparents on his wicker nightstand flipped down. So he righted it. The next day, the photo was facing down again. Later that morning, after leaving his room for breakfast, he returned and found in the middle of his bed two Beanie Babies — the zebra and the tiger — next to a conch shell, a dinosaur made of shells and a plaster toucan bird.

That got his parents' — and his twin brother, Lee's — attention.

Trying to make sense of the irrational, Al called out, "Do we have a Casper here? Tell me your name and how old you are." Then he left some lined composition paper and crayons and, with his family, walked out of the room.

In 15 minutes they returned and found written vertically in large block childlike letters, "Danny, 7."

See **DANNY**, Page 8C

Danny's writings

Boy: Ghost in my bed

Jane Fishman talks
with a family who says
they have experienced
paranormal activities
in their house. **1C**

Danny

Continued from page 1C

The next day — before the boys
went to Savannah Arts Academy,
where they're in the ninth grade,
and their mother, Lila, went to
work in a construction company
office — Al asked, "Tell me if you
have any connection to the antique
oak bed and when you may have
died."

A few hours later, when they
returned to the room, the slanted
stick letters said, "Mom — sick in
bed. Died 1899. Lov (sic) toys." And
piled on the bed were Lila's senior
picture from Savannah Christian,
an electric foot massage, a can of
fish food and more toys.

That night, when he was sleeping, Jason heard a loud bang. When
he woke up he saw a pole lamp on
its side, a child's terra cotta head
that had fallen off the wall, some
scattered pencils and the words,
"Mean man."

"He was trying to get our attention," said Al, who also graduated
from Savannah Christian. "None of
us ever felt he meant any harm. But
believe me, nothing like this ever
happened before."

In the next few days, there were
more exchanges. A note — "Want to
stay with bed. Saw mom." A pile of
personal effects — four of Sir
Walter Scott's Waverly novels,
which Jason kept on his desk,
stacked on a wicker trunk, broken
glass in the photo of Lila's grandparents, photographs of Al's sisters
when they were 6 and 7, one of
Lila's mixing bowls, a yellow bird
figurine from the dining room, a
red clay angel from the kitchen.

And more communiques.

When Lila asked, "Why did you
break my parents' picture?" the
note read, "Sorry Lila." When Al
queried, "Don't you want to cross
over and go see your mom?" he
found, "Want to stay with bed. Saw
mom." To Al's question "Can you
see my father and tell him I love
him?" and "What's your last name?
Where do you come from?" he
learned, "Tired sorry Al no connet
(sic) yet" and "Secret Al."

For a week, the Cobbs were curious, open and believing. That
"Danny" — whose soul, Al theo-
rized, had become absorbed in the
wood of the bed — was trying to
make friends with them.

But then things turned sour. The
same day they found a note reading, "No one sleep in bed," Jason,
who had moved out of the room,
decided to stretch out and pretend
to take a nap.

That, says Al, was a mistake.

"I doubled back in the room to
pick up my clothes," remembers
Jason, "when this terra cotta head
that had been hanging on the wall
came flying through the room, just
missing me before it smashed on
the closet door."

That's when Lila said, "OK, that's
it. Everyone out of the house. I
want this bed out, too."

No one argued. Al moved the bed
to the garage and after wavering
for a few days, hauled it off to
Kramer and Sadler Auctions. When
the bed left, "Danny" left.

"The whole thing was stressful,"
Al said. "It was like having a
kindergartner loose in your home
when you're not there. You don't
know what to think. We really
believe we had a little guy in our
house, a 'stay behind,' as some people call them.

"But I couldn't let a ghost, or
whatever, take over my son's room.
I had to go with the living."

**Jane Fishman's column appears
Wednesday, Friday and Sunday. She
can be reached at (912) 652-0313.
At our web site,
www.savannahnow.com, you can e-
mail Jane or catch up on some of her
past columns.**

We know where his bed is — but where's Danny?

Andy Kramer will auction Danny's bed at Kramer & Sadler Auctions Inc. on Monday.

Jane Fishman

Al Cobb was there — with written updates from "Danny."

So was the couple from the D & D Old Timey Shop in Pembroke who bought the bed from Cobb at auction. So was the financial manager from Southern Motors who bought the bed several days later at the couple's shop in Pembroke. So was the Chatham County vice squad detective who bought the bed from the financial manager at Monday night's auction.

But where was "Danny?"

We don't know.

We don't know a lot when it comes to the paranormal, the spirit world, the supernatural.

But we'd like to.

At least that's my take on the matter, 10 days — and at least 50 queries later by phone, fax, mail, radio and in person over the vegetables at the supermarket — after writing about one family's experience with a turn-of-the-century honey-oak antique bed and a presence named "Danny."

Cobb, who owns Cobb's Galleries on Whitaker Street, bought the bed for $120 several weeks ago from Savannah Auction for his teen-age son, Jason, who likes antiques. Several nights later, when Jason said he felt as if someone were watching him, Cobb and his wife, Lila, put out pencil and paper and a slew of questions. When they returned to the room, they found "Danny, 7" written in large block-style lettering.

The notes continued. So did toys in the bed, photographs turned upside down, mixing bowls moved from kitchen to bedroom. The family was interested, willing to suspend disbelief. But when a terracotta angel flew off the wall and nearly hit Jason, Lila said, "That's it. Danny's got to go."

See FISHMAN, Page 3C

33

Continued from page 1C

Al wrapped up the bed and took it to Kramer & Sadler Auctions.

That Monday, when Debra Brogdon — who knew nothing about "Danny" and already had one foot out the door — heard the bed come up for bid, she turned to her husband, David, last year's Teacher of the Year from Windsor Forest High School, and said, "I want that bed." They paid $60.

The next day Cobb called to tell them what else they may have purchased — so did six other people desperate to own the bed. The Brogdons had no intention of selling. They talked of building a bedroom especially for "Danny."

But the calls were staggering. So were the freaked-out reactions of customers who refused to enter the Brogdons' store when they heard the story. And the negative response of David's sister who said she didn't want her relatives messing with spirits.

So the couple relented and sold the bed for $200 to Faith Dismukh from Southern Motors. She thought it might look good in her third bedroom. After three days of no

response and no "Danny," she said she felt lonely. Last Friday she brought it back to Kramer's.

The following Saturday, Sunday and Monday, auctioneer/former Andy Kramer said the building's motion detector — not the alarm — kept blinking. That same weekend an unset alarm clock went off at the Brogdons' shop.

And Al and Lila, feeling "Danny" might still be in their house, recorded a few more conversations. To their question, "What else do you want?" they learned, "Danny go up by by (sic)." To "Why did you not stay with bed?" they read, "Lady sold me. Mean lady."

After Al decided to listen to his wife and sons and not accept an offer to appear on local television, they received a note that read, "Danny happy. Al mean. Listen to family."

their question, "What else do you want?" they learned, "Danny go up by by (sic)." To "Why did you not stay with bed?" they read, "Lady sold me. Mean lady."

The first three hours of Monday night's auction proceeded on schedule. A Victorian parlor chair. Two bisque and porcelain figurines. Eight blue willow plates. Five sherbet bowls. But that was before the announcement, which quieted the room as fast as a devil at a Baptist revival.

"All right, ladies and gentlemen. I make no claims for this bed," said Kramer, who majored in journalism at Boston College. "You all know me pretty well. I don't lie. Well, maybe I stretch the truth a little. But we're not here to deceive you. And I do have a fiduciary responsibility to my customers."

Then, the microphone covering his mouth, Kramer upped the rhythm, moved into auctionese and jokingly started the bid at $5,000. Minutes later, buyer No. 28, Detective Joey Warsznak, who

moonlights at the auction house and plans to sell the bed through the Internet, topped the five-person contest at $525.

"I'm not sure what I believe about all this," Warsznak said afterward. "I do," Debra Brogdon said. "I still think he's in my shop."

Jane Fishman's column appears on Wednesday, Friday and Sunday. She can be reached at 652-0313. At our web site, www.savannahnow.com, you can e-mail Jane or catch up on some of her past columns.

were involved with paranormal entities. There are a dozen G host Haunting Tours taking place in Savannah on any given day of the week. These locations have been documented by some of the most well-known paranormal investigators in the world. Dozens of books have also been written about Savannah ghosts and poltergeists.

At the time, I talked with one of WTOC's reporters, a woman named Elaine, who wanted to come over and do the story immediately, but she had prior commitments, so I was to be interviewed by Jason Rockwell the following morning.

I was excited about all the potentials, but neither Lila nor the boys wanted to do the story and declined to be interviewed.

Lila and the boys felt that if our story was shown on television that they would be teased unmercifully at school. But, in truth, when the story did eventually come out, their close friends thought that their experiences were cool. Within an hour after I told them of the potential interview, Lila and Jason found another note from "Danny." This time the note read: "Danny Happy," "Al Mean," "Listen to Family." I couldn't afford to get on the wrong side of my family's wishes, nor "Danny's," since there were still many things I wished to learn from him. I was outnumbered and outgunned, so ten minutes later I called the TV station and canceled the interview.

"Danny" continued to communicate with us about those conversations he overheard. On one occasion, he gave some friendly advice to one of our sons. The last person I ever thought my wife and I would catch smoking was our son Lee. Both of Lila's parents and my father died from lung cancer, so we hold no love for the tobacco industry. Lee was caught flatfooted and red-handed with matches and cigarettes. We were both stunned that he would ever place a cigarette in his mouth, so we called him out on the carpet and crawled all over him for his stupidity. Since "Danny" could clearly hear us bringing Lee down a notch or two, it wasn't long before we received another note: "Lee, Stop, Please," he wrote.

The woman who bought "Danny's" bed from the dealers in Pembroke only kept it in her garage for less than a week, and then it went back to the Kramer/Sadler Auction House. Lila was thinking of bidding on the bed and buying it back for "Danny," so she wrote him a note. "Is it okay to let the bed go?" she asked. "Danny" replied in short order, "Yes!"

On the evening of October 27, 1998, Jason was standing in front of his desk having completed his homework that night when he noticed his curtains suddenly released themselves from their tiebacks and they continued moving until they closed tightly. He watched this happen unbelievingly and reopened the curtains and tied them back again. The very same thing happened and he raced upstairs to find another witness and I happened to be available. When I walked in his room, I saw the pulls and the curtains moving as well. The only other physical object that was found out of place that night was a seashell that sat across the room from its normal position beside the fish tank.

Jason was awakened at midnight by the sound of his closet door opening and then closing. He sat up and looked across the room and spotted the shadow of a little boy moving as if on tip toe in front of his closet door. Jason called out to the little shadow figure, "Danny, is that you?" The image froze in place as if playing a game of freeze tag. No response to the question was made as the shadow quickly disappeared into the surface of the closet door.

The following night, at nine o'clock, we received a call from a representative of Fox TV. Her name was Sabrina Bonnet, and she asked about doing a national story about "Danny" and the haunted bed. I told her that my family and I were still on the fence about where to take the story since none of us wanted people to think we were crazy for believing in these paranormal experiences. She gave me her number, and I told her I would call her back after we had a family conference.

Lila walked into Jason's room and spoke out loud to "Danny" and asked him if it were he who was in front of Jason's closet at midnight. I walked in the room behind her and left a note asking if he wanted to be a star on FOX TV in California. "Danny" soon wrote back, "ME CLOSET" in answer to Lila and "NO, BUT TELL STORY," in response to my note to him.

Much to Jason's chagrin he learned that what "Danny" had meant in his earlier note to us about going "UP, BY, BY," was that he now sleeps above Jason. Over time, Lila had two more questions for "Danny." The first one was simply whether "Danny" had anything to say to Jason. "Danny's" response to this question was "SORRY, JASON." The second question was, "Where do you sleep?" "Danny" drew a happy pumpkin in the spirit of the upcoming Halloween season, and he wrote again, "ABOVE JASON."

Jason and Lee always love the Halloween season, and Lila and I let the boys decorate the house in all their favorite ghouls and goblins. "All Hallows Eve" has always been for me the most fun that I can remember as a kid. My friends and I covered many different neighborhoods and collected two full grocery bags of Halloween treats each. I always had plenty of candy till after Christmas. We always stayed out all night and each new neighborhood we went to was a little more alien than the next, and this unfamiliarity added to the weird atmosphere of the event. Sometimes we covered over two miles as we circled through many different close-knit subdivisions. We were bushed when we finally would get home, but two sacks of candy would cover the labor we put in to the hunt.

That season Jason and Lee did a fabulous job inside and outside our house with their "Halloween Magic." The house had tape recorders playing ghostly music with sounds of chains rattling and people moaning and screaming. The front porch was lined with two standing zombies and a man sitting in one corner whose one eye watched you as you neared the door looking for treats. In the front yard they had a cemetery complete with moss-covered tombstones and gates. They used yards of cobwebs with spiders and other creepy crawly things in their work. Each year they get a little better.

My niece, Amber Ledlow, spent Halloween night with us and she and my sons went out trick or treating together. We had told her about our poltergeist and she offered to leave out a package of M&M's and a miniature Hershey bar for him to open. The next day both packages were opened and their contents spilled out on the top of the trunk at the foot of Jason's bed where we left them. Lila found them opened after we both had been monitoring the room that day, and "Danny" had not touched them. We could now call Amber and tell her that "Danny" liked his candy.

The following day I tried to get "Danny" to visit my Grandmother Cobb who had passed away about six years after my dad. "Please tell her I love and miss her," I told "Danny" as I left a photograph of my grandmother and myself taken in 1960. I called Jason from work and asked him if he would check the message that I left for "Danny" to see if there was any answer. I waited and Jason returned to the phone and told me "Yes, there is Daddy". "DON'T KNOW" was all he wrote.

When I got home that evening I had a brainstorm. Why not challenge "Danny" to an old fashioned game of Tic-Tac-Toe? Just Jason and I were home at this time, so I explained to Jason what I wanted to do and I had him draw the grid lines for the game with "Danny." "Danny's" presence could be felt in the room with us so we told him that Jason would play him the first game as "X's" and that he would be "O's." Jason made the first move by leaving an X in the lower left-hand corner of the grid. Then we both walked out of the room to give "Danny" a chance to reply. As we were passing through the dining room, the kitchen door opened and Lila and Lee returned from the mall. She asked me if "Danny' was up to anything since they had left, and I told her that Jason and I were trying an experimental Tick-Tac-Toe game with "Danny" in Jason's room. The words were no more out of my mouth than Lila had to go see for herself if "Danny" had made his mark yet. "Al, come back here right now!" she exclaimed. When both Jason and I joined her and Lee in the room, we all saw what "Danny" had marked on the sheet. "Danny" had taken all three of his "O" moves at once, and then struck a line through them writing "HA! HA!"

Jason told "Danny" that he could only make one move at a time and drew a new grid for the second game allowing "Danny' to make the first move this time. "Danny" made no response to this game, so after twenty minutes Lila made three "X's" and crossed through them and then asked "Danny" if he wanted a second chance to play her. She wrote, "I win, 'Danny'" beside the grid. Lila made the grid for the third game and placed an "X" at the bottom center square. At a quarter past nine, Lila checked to see how the game was going and "Danny" had again made three "O" moves at once and wrote, "HA!, HA!, BEAT YOU!"

On another occasion "Danny" demonstrated his ability to communicate about knowledge on this plane. My birthday was approaching in just two days, and Lila asked me what kind of party I would like. My normal style of birthday party is pretty standard. Lila makes me an upside down pineapple cake, and we have immediate family over for ice cream and fruit punch mixed with ginger ale. I open my gifts, the kids play with games and toys, and the adults have a little coffee and conversation.

No one had mentioned how old I would be on my upcoming birthday but "Danny" knew. Downstairs was a letter sheet that read, "HAPP B DAY AL 45" in colored pencil. Here was another astonishing communiqué from the other side, but by now it had begun to seem commonplace.

Of everyone attempting to communicate with "Danny," Jason has perhaps the most direct path. Since the beginning of "Danny's" entry into our house and lives, Jason has been able to feel the moment he arrives from the other side. He gets a weird electric feel and popping sound in his head that is like a fingerprint of "Danny's" presence. When "Danny" first arrived, we thought he only played with Jason's earthly toys in the room, but "Danny" also brought with him three toys that were special to him in his previous life. This is the second way that Jason can pinpoint "Danny's" whereabouts in a flash. Like a bell on a cat, "Danny's" toys make a sound that Jason can pick up instantly. The two Victorian pull toys that "Danny" plays with are a stuffed horse with metal wheels and a big Spanish-

American tin battleship on wheels. Both toys and a large spinning top are the sounds Jason's ears pick up when he hears "Danny" playing in the closet, the attic, or anywhere else in the house.

I had been asked by several people if "Danny" could possibly know what is going to happen in the future. Could he pick out a winning lottery number or tell us if a negative occurrence was heading our way? The answer is no. We had been asked by the Catholic priest to ask "Danny" once again if he wanted to go into the light, but for the second time he let us know that he had seen Jesus and been to the other side, and he is happy and okay. Been there and done that seemed to be the order of the day, and yet most spirits return to earth for some kind of unfinished business. "Danny" just hasn't let us in on what that is just yet.

When my birthday arrived, I dropped by the Kramer/Sadler auction house, and I talked to the new owner of "Danny's" bed, Joey Warenzak. Joey is a Chatham County Police detective and often helps out at the auction house. He bought the bed on Monday night's auction for $550.00 and thought he was making a good investment since the bed was becoming so well known. He was more than a little interested in knowing what "Danny" felt about him since he was the bed's new owner. In the few days he had owned the bed, he told me he had taken it to his Wilmington Island home and set it up in his garage. He told me that he can feel himself being constantly watched and that his dog growls at the bed constantly.

Joey asked me if I would please leave "Danny" a note and ask him if he knew him as the present owner of the bed and how he felt about him. "Danny" was already upset about his bed going from our house to the auction house and then to two more people after that, so he wasn't exactly complimentary concerning Joey when he answered my question. "Do you know Joey W., the new owner of your bed?" I asked. "Danny" wrote back, "Yes, Stupid, Ha!, Ha!, Ha!" I got back the following day with Joey and showed him the note that "Danny" had written. He simply laughed it off. I want to point out that from my standpoint it was embarrassing for me to give Joey the news. But being the good natured and competent police officer that he is, he was trying his best to communicate with "Danny" too. I promised to keep him informed if "Danny" had anything else to say.

The following Saturday I began my routine of getting out and about to the yard sales and estate sales. I was busy cleaning, recording, and organizing that morning's finds at my antique shop when Lila called. "Guess what", she said. "Danny" has been really opening up to us this morning."

Lila had gone to the drugstore earlier and purchased a child's book called "While I Sleep" by Mary Calhoun. She had felt compelled to buy the brightly colored children's book for "Danny." She noticed the cover of the book showed a young boy about "Danny's" age sleeping on a bed and dreaming. Inside were toys from the same time period and the character's feelings for the mother figure in the book were very similar to the way "Danny" felt about his mom.

She didn't go into the drugstore to buy the book, and yet it seemed to garner her attention. The moment she skimmed through it she knew it was just the right prescription for "Danny." When she arrived home and laid out her purchases on the kitchen counter, she removed the book from the bag and placed the book on the wooden tea cart in the living room. She announced to "Danny" the fact that she had bought it for him and went about her weekend chores. Lila had opened the book to the first chapter and then left the room to do housework. Each time she came back through the living room the pages had moved forward. One moment it was on a page with a cat and the next it was on a page with a train engine. It was obvious that "Danny" had taken to and was enjoying his book. "Danny" wrote Lila a note in big letters telling her "THANK YOU LILA FOR BOOK."

We had a coloring book contest for the children and adults at my party the night before and each of us did a little art work for prizes. We saved one out on the table "just in case" "Danny" were to show up. I even invited him to help me blow out my candles too. The following evening he had written to Lee and Jason about, and given us a description of, his toys. He also indicated that he is capable of going anywhere on earth. Another note was left out for me saying, "Sorry Al Was Too Far Away Happy B-Day."

The picture I had left out for "Danny" to color was a happy bear floating through the air with four balloons pulling him skyward. Eventually, we found the little work of art fully colored in and signed "Danny." This was the best job I ever saw a spirit do and I would not sell it for a million dollars! To me, it is as unique as the Mona Lisa or Whistler's Mother.

Danny colored in and signed this "Happy Bear" the day after my birthday November 7, 1998.

Danny loved to color, as was evidenced by us finding the dining room chair just slightly turned at an angle where we usually laid out the crayons and coloring books for his pleasure. This happened several times. On other occasions, we found the little shell dinosaur on the table holding crayons in his arms.

When we first brought the bed home from the auction, I did my best trying to find out its origins. I contacted an auction house in Darlington, South Carolina, who had sold it to the Savannah Auction Galleries. They led me to a grandmother who called me from Wilmington, North Carolina. She told me that her grandbaby had slept on it for a while before it ended up in the dealer auction in Darlington. Now, all day long, there seemed to be no end to the information that "Danny" was giving Lila and the boys while I sat at work. He still would not give out any information on what the face of God looked like or anything about his father which he referred to as a "Mean Man."

"Danny" did write Lila and the boys that he was from North Carolina, but left out the specific city. He lived in a two story mansion which explains how he happened to have nice toys. Possibly, it meant that he came from a wealthy family. He wrote that he visits his mom on the other side and when he peers into a mirror he sees himself as a brown-haired and brown-eyed seven-year-old. Later in the evening, when I was home, Jason came into the kitchen and showed Lila something else that "Danny" was up to now. Jason was missing the shell-covered dinosaur from his dresser and was searching his room when he spied it on top of the ceiling fan. They both called me into the room a few moments later and told me that "Danny" was playing "Hide and Seek" with Jason's dinosaur and asked me if I saw where he had hidden it. I looked all over the room but missed it. Lila said, "look up," and I could barely see it standing behind one of the fan blades. I wrote him a note and told him what a clever hiding place he had chosen and he wrote back "HA, HA!"

Since "Danny" had played a joke on me, I thought I would try another angle with him. I wanted in the worst way to get some sort of video tape of him in our home or some decent photographs for evidence. I kept a camera and a video at arms length at all times. I thought I would ask "Danny" if he would play a game of Tic-Tac-Toe with me and if I won I would get to take his picture and if he won he would get to close the window curtains in front of the video camera. "NO!" was all he wrote. Never try to fool a spirit or at least come up with a better plan than I did. I did apologize and played a game of Tic-Tac-Toe with "Danny" in which he did the same thing to me as all the others and took his three turns after my one and just to rub it in a little further he wrote, "HA!"

Later that same night, "Danny" answered several questions that both Lee and Jennifer had posed to him. "Yes, Yes, Lee, I can fly around in the sky, but not where the stars are," and "PLEASE TELL JENNIFER STOP SMOKING!" To Jennifer he noted, "Hay, JENNIFER!" and "YES!" to the fact that he has brothers and sisters, "ALL DIED," he concluded.

The most fantastic incident that "Danny" led my family through concerned the spirit of another Savannah child whose monument stands today at The Bonaventure Cemetery. That Saturday, on November 7, I was making the rounds as usual to the estate and yard sales. It was a beautiful, sunny Savannah morning and everything was bright, cheery and comfortable. I went to the annual Benedictine Military School Rummage Sale held in the massive school cafeteria. While searching through a pile of cookbooks on a round card table, I noticed a little 6-3/4 X 5" photo for ten cents. I dropped it in my box with the cookbooks and other items I purchased. The photo turned out to be one of the kind that are sold in gift shops to tourists in Savannah, Georgia. It was from a series of note cards from "The Bonaventure Series at Bonaventure Cemetery" by a photographer who signed them "Bonita".

The photograph was of a little girl seated on a marble pedestal with her hand resting on the stump of a live tree symbolizing the short life of a beautiful young child. Her name was Gracie Watson. She was the only child of Mr. W.J. Watson and his wife Frances. Her daddy was the manager of The Pulaski Hotel that stood on the corner of Bull and Bryan streets just down from city hall in the bustling times of the 1880's. It stood overlooking Johnson square as one of Savannah's best known landmarks. It is the present site of the Piccadilly Restaurant.

Little Gracie was a great ambassador for her father's hotel, and the Patrons of the Pulaski loved her greeting them with her sweet, smiling face and the flowers she gave them. Gracie loved to play with toys and pick fresh flowers. She especially loved to ride on the train to Tybee Beach with her dad on his days off. At six years old in 1889, she contracted pneumonia and died in her father's arms. Her last question to her grieving father was, "Daddy, do they have trains in heaven?"

The Savannah Morning News recorded that on the day of Little Gracie's funeral there were hundreds of mourners in the parlor of the Pulaski Hotel. She was eulogized and taken to Bonaventure Cemetery for burial. Mr. Watson and his wife Frances were never the same after the death of their "Little Princess." Money was being raised to build a monument to "Little Gracie" and the only photograph of Gracie that the father owned was handed to the greatest sculptor Savannah had ever known, John Walz.

As he handed the photograph to the artist, the father was so grievous at the loss of his daughter that all words failed him as he walked away. John Walz sensed that this artwork would be one of the most important of any work he had ever done as he set to work on what was to become his masterpiece. When the statue was unveiled, all of Savannah turned out and "Little Gracie" was now a treasure for the ages. She is the most visited statue of a child than any other in the South.

When I came home that afternoon, I called everyone into the kitchen to tell them about the finds I made that morning and to show them the picture I found of "Little Gracie Watson." I left the photograph standing on the kitchen counter and we all went upstairs to watch a movie I brought home.

"Danny know Gracie, Friend" was written on a sheet on the back of Jason's trunk. He brought it to Lila and me to read. I could only guess that child spirits who still possibly roam the earth may meet each other and become kindred spirits. After all, "Danny" was only seven when he died and "Little Gracie" was only six. He may look at her as a little sister. Who knows? "Tomorrow morning, we are going to take a ride over to Bonaventure Cemetery," I told the family.

The following Sunday morning Lila, Jason, and I arrived at the earliest time possible just after they opened the gates. Lee stayed home and slept in. I noticed as we were driving through the cemetery that there were many more fine statues that John Walz had done that are incredibly beautiful. Over seventy statues and architectural works of art have been identified as his in Savannah, Georgia, but "little "Gracie" is his best known.

After we had visited the Cobb family plot in the Greenwich section, we turned the car southward and headed for the "Gracie Section." It didn't take us long as we followed the narrow moss-lined oak tree path till we spotted a little, white-arrow marker saying "Gracie Section." I parked on the narrow pathway in front of the beloved statue, and the three of us introduced ourselves as we stood in front of the child. "We are friends of "Danny," I told her, "and he tells us that you and he are friends and we are happy to meet you." Jason told Lila and me that he felt that the spirit of the little girl was looking out at us that very moment. I could see how hauntingly beautiful she was as I touched the cool marble locks on her head. "Do you mind if we take your picture, Gracie?" I asked. So I snapped about four or five different angles, and we said goodbye and left.

Danny had a spiritual connection to Gracie Watson and wrote he knew her. She passed away at the tender age of 6 in 1889.

I have learned since attending a meeting of the "Friends of Bonaventure" that one should not allow one's skin to come into contact with the marble sculptures because the salt in a person's fingertips and the acid rain can mix with other pollutants to cause a physical breakdown of both cement and marble. The marble then becomes very brittle and fragile and eventually the statue breaks down and withers away. Since the time we last visited "Gracie," she has now been enclosed in a protective iron and bronze fence that is designed to protect her from both vandals and those who simply wish to touch her.

On the morning we visited "Gracie," we noticed that she had a fresh cut flower cupped in her hand. There were no footprints in the grass around her, nor was there a hint that anyone had preceded us to visit her that morning. How did that fresh flower come to be in her hand? I had talked earlier on the phone to a local Savannah psychic who told me that she sees "Little Gracie" playing in the cemetery every time she visits. She is running around unbeknownst to those who don't have "the sight." The psychic sees her in her high-buttoned shoes and bright Victorian dress, picking flowers as she dances and plays around those visiting their deceased family members. She always carries with her a bouquet of fresh cut flowers.

At ten o'clock that evening, we sent Jason to bed since it was a school night. A few minutes later he came back upstairs and informed Lila and me that "Danny" was in his room that very moment. I said, "Jason, what's so unusual about that? You know he told us that he sleeps above you." "It's not one set of eyes watching me tonight," he replied. " There are two sets of eyes watching me!"

I asked Jason if he were making this up, but he said, "No, Dad. One of the spirits I feel is "Danny" and the other spirit is a smaller, younger, female spirit. I think it's 'Gracie!'" Lila and I just looked at each other in utter amazement! She walked downstairs with Jason to his room to try to calm him down and what she witnessed convinced her that spirits really do exist around us in our everyday lives. She was standing over him and speaking with him when she caught the strange movement of a napkin at the head of his bed, quietly floating upward and unfolding itself. Then, as it drifted downward, it folded itself back up again. That napkin literally danced on the pillows in front of her! Jason, noticing his mother's perplexed expression told her she wasn't seeing things and that he could feel the breeze from both spirits at the head of the bed as they romped and played together. No heat or air was on when this event happened, and we could not explain it other than a visit from not one, but two poltergeists.

I walked downstairs just moments after Lila had seen the napkins dance. "They're upstairs playing in the attic too," Jason told us. I went back upstairs to see what he could be talking about and, sure enough, both "Danny" and "Gracie" had been playing there. A small Christmas tree was moved on top of an old mattress that we had stored there and other holiday items were out of place.

When Lila and I did talk Jason into going back downstairs to his bedroom for some sleep, he couldn't because he could hear them talking in loud whispers and the sound of toys moving behind the closed, closet door kept him up all night. This was confirmed the following morning as we opened Jason's closet door and everything was out of whack.

Chapter Two

A New Spirit Makes His Way Into Our Home

On the fifth of January, 1999, Lila and I went to our respective jobs, she to her job as an office manager of a local construction company and I to my job as the owner/operator of an antiques shop. Jason and Lee had gone to school and things began to settle back to a normal everyday schedule. I had no way of knowing we were in for a rude awakening.

Lila received a call from Mrs. Norton, the school nurse at The Savannah Arts Academy, saying that Jason was not feeling well, so Lila picked him up at school. Within an hour after she dropped him off at the house, he called me at my shop and, in a shaky voice, said, "Dad, there is another spirit in our house."

Jason had been lying down when he began to sense a different buzzing sound in his head than that of "Danny's" lower-volume buzzing sound. When he arose from the couch, he began to hear more muted thumping and bumping sounds downstairs and a steady tread of someone's footsteps. He quietly tip-toed downstairs to investigate who or what was the source. At first, he didn't see anything as he peered into the living room from the adjacent hallway, but the sounds continued as if the house were alive.

The sounds were no longer in his head, but ebbed and flowed throughout the house. Jason reached his hand out and around the corner and grabbed the kitchen phone that was hanging there and dialed my number. When I answered the phone in my office, I felt terrified as he described in great detail the new spirit, and, through the phone lines, I shared his fearful emotions. I felt an odd nervous twitch in my chest and butterflies in my stomach as he gave a blow-by-blow account of what he witnessed in the living room.

Rising up from the fireplace, some twenty feet away, was a tall, husky nineteenth-century mountain man! He was wearing a long, grey knee- length jacket with bright, shiny brass buttons. His dark, black boots were pulled up over his brown pants. His face was weathered and craggy from years of living a rugged, outdoor life. His eyes were a clear, brilliant blue. His nose was narrow and his long hair was salt and pepper grey. He wore a tall beaver-skin hat with a long, white plumb trailing down. In many ways, he looked like the famous American symbol "Uncle Sam" in mountaineers' clothing, rather than the traditional red, white, and blue suit.

The black boots that "Uncle Sam" wore made a loud, scraping sound as he stood, now fully materialized in front of the fireplace. For five minutes, Jason watched the spirit standing at the fireplace. He was stunned at the length of time this spirit remained in material form. Our little dog, "Lady," came downstairs barking and snapping at the phantom figure, but he paid little attention to her as he kept studying the mother and child portrait we have hanging over the mantle. He kept his back turned to Jason as he walked along the fireplace wall and studied each item. Then, as if he were standing inside a museum, he examined the furniture and fireplace tools.

"Uncle Sam" had not turned his face towards Jason since he first materialized from the fireplace, but, suddenly, he glanced towards Jason and Lady and vanished! I could hear Lady barking on the phone, and Jason told me the man had disappeared. Lady is a crossbreed of a poodle and a schnauzer, we call her a "Snoodle." She has proven to us that she also has the ability to see and hear any spirits that have found their way into our home. She will stand perfectly still and her ears will stand straight up as she just listens for awhile without moving a muscle. She has also taken off like a jet when she spots one of the spirits traveling through our home.

I stayed on the line with Jason during this bizarre episode and I asked him, "Jason, are you okay?" "Yes," he replied. "He's gone now." I offered to come home right then, but he said he would be fine and promised to call me back if "Uncle Sam" returned. In the next few moments, I was busy answering several customer calls and, since I don't have "call waiting," Jason could not get through when he tried moments later.

Jason tried to call me minutes after I last spoke to him. "Uncle Sam" had only vanished temporarily and was moving through the house like a lightening bolt, opening up cabinets and pulling out china cabinet drawers, all simultaneously and in every room throughout the house! An invisible specter moving around you at great speed can be much more frightening than the calm spirit Jason witnessed earlier near the fireplace. He called Lila at work and told her that all the cabinets and drawers had opened up in front of him, and she told him to gather Lady up into his arms and leave the house immediately.

The phone rang at my office seconds after talking with one of my customers. It was Lila, and she said in a commanding voice, "Jason needs you! Go home right now!" I closed my shop and headed out the door.

Back at the house, Jason was holding Lady in his arms and still talking to Lila on the kitchen phone when he heard loud resounding footsteps coming down the stairs behind him. They got closer and closer, and he knew that something was standing directly behind him, but he saw nothing. At that moment he felt a large hand grab him by the arm, and he passed out and lay in a heap on the floor. The telephone was dangling from the wall and the room was quiet. Lila called out to Jason, but there was no answer.

I set another new speed record as I raced home down the Harry Truman Parkway at 90 miles per hour. I was just hoping that one of Chatham County's finest would follow me but not today of all days. I pulled into the driveway and jumped out of the car like a maniac and ran to the front door. My front door key acted like it was too big for the lock, but I finally got it to fit. When I opened the door, everything was topsy-turvy. It really appeared as if someone were searching the house for valuables or a whole gang of burglars had invaded our home and trashed everything.

I called out for Jason three times and got no answer. My heart was beating faster and faster as I searched for him in his room and in Lee's room. I came back through the living room to the kitchen and found Jason wrapped in a blanket face down on the floor. A cane-seated chair lay on top of him. I managed to get him back to consciousness and, although groggy, he said he felt this spirit was still in the house.

I picked up the phone and called 911 and requested police officers to come as soon as possible. In about seven minutes, a new white Chatham County police car pulled in at the far end of our fifty-five foot driveway to try, I guess, to reconnoiter the situation. It's not every day, an officer gets a call from a fanatical father whose son has been attacked by a spirit!

The officer seemed to be a little unsure as to whether or not he would make the initial contact by himself on this call. I saw him sitting out in the driveway, and so I walked out to meet him halfway to put any fears he had to rest. He did eventually walk through the house with me, and he questioned Jason about what caused him to pass out. The doors and windows were all locked and secured from inside. Nothing was missing and only a single red Christmas candle was damaged. It had been stepped on near the fireplace.

I showed the officer a series of signed prints we had lining the stairway that had been all turned to right angles. A very heavy green imitation Christmas tree that we had upstairs in the window of the bonus room was spirited downstairs in the spot that earlier held our white Christmas tree. It takes two people to move that tree with the stand and lights, and yet here it was downstairs and plugged in and ready to use.

The Franciscan Apple china was removed from several cabinets, and the table was set for six, as if the spirit wished to share a Christmas dinner with us after the holiday. An old mahogany box, filled with a 1920's silver-plated flatware service for eight, was sitting opened and spread out on the table. Six places were set following the proper etiquette for soup and desert. Neither Jason nor Lee have ever been taught how to set a table in such a way. Since Lila and I don't entertain with formal dinners, they never learned how.

The door bell rang and the second officer stepped into the house, and his partner filled him in on his investigation. We showed him the upstairs and downstairs as well. Basically, nothing was stolen and Jason seemed to be all right now, so we began at once to discuss how my report should be handled. "Mr. Cobb," he began, "if I were you, I wouldn't make this preliminary report official." "Why?" I asked. "Well," they advised, "once we make it official, the newspaper reporters will pick the story up off the police blotter and you will have all kinds of strange people hanging around your house!" I agreed with them and never made an official report.

The following night things had settled down somewhat and Lila was balancing her checkbooks and handling other important household paperwork when I walked by her sitting at the kitchen table. I said, "Lila, what in the world is my *World-Wide Guide To Nudist Colonies* book sitting out in the middle of the table?" She responded, "What nudist book?" I told her, "It's the book sitting out in front of you. "How did it get here?" "I had it hidden in the closet, so the boys wouldn't find it." It's just an old, softbound book that I purchased from a yard sale because I thought it was such a hoot. I long ago had tossed it into the back of my closet. The boys denied ever knowing about it, and I believe them since they were upstairs on the computer that entire evening while Lila sat at the table. We believe that "Uncle Sam" spirited it out of my closet because he thought it was hilarious too.

I don't claim to be a psychic, but the most peculiar feeling came over me while I sat upstairs watching Dennis Hopper on an HBO movie called *Space Truckers*. My ears suddenly felt as if they were filling up with water, and the sounds around me were being absorbed. A strange popping sound, followed by a buzzing one, seemed to overtake my thoughts, and this sensation diverted my attention to the feeling that someone was in my room opening up my dresser. I told Lila and the boys that I felt "Uncle Sam" in my room!" The boys said, "Sure, Dad...," like they didn't believe me, so I got up and went downstairs to check. I called to them back upstairs and invited them to see what had taken place in my room. My dresser had all the drawers pulled out in an even graduated pattern. I set out some paper and pens for "Uncle Sam" to communicate with us, but so far he hasn't. I think it will just be a matter of time before he does. He has been searching our house from top to bottom for something.

Eight days later, we almost had a duplication of the events of the previous week. Jason had a doctor's appointment so instead of taking him back to school Lila dropped him off at home since school was near-

ly out for the day. She was down the road, heading back to work when Jason heard the cabinets popping open again downstairs. This time, I left the store and raced home in ten minutes, remembering what had happened the previous week. The moment he called I knew there was no time to waste since this spirit works incredibly fast.

Almost the same identical stuff that happened before, happened again. The pictures were all turned at right angles. The Franciscan Apple china was back out on the table, except only the small desert bowls were out as if we were going to have fruit or berries. The silver-plate was spread out on the table, but this time only the desert spoons lay beside each bowl.

More unusual things happened this time as well. The living room pictures were switched with the pictures in the dining room and the light bulbs had been unscrewed from the electrical sockets in the chandelier over the kitchen table. The bulbs and the blown glass shades were left lying out on top of the table.

We often found furniture drawers left open throughout the house. This is a sample of what the spirits did with my highboy.

Ten feet up on a shelf in our living room, every "Gone with the Wind" lamp that we had in the house was lined up side by side. It took Jason and me both to get them down with a ten foot ladder! Jason had watched "Uncle Sam" materialize upstairs while he was on the phone calling Lila. As he spoke to her on the phone, she could hear the spirit tossing VHS movies off the shelf and knocking over the oak office chair we have upstairs.

This time Jason took refuge under a heavy English pub table that we use to keep our home computer and printer on. He stayed on the phone with Lila until all phones went dead at her construction company. He remembered what I had said to him a few days before and called out to "Uncle Sam": "In the name of Jesus Christ, leave this house!" The spirit ceased his destruction and turned and waved to Jason as he floated by and then he passed through the solid wood of the attic door!

Jason began to breathe a little easier, thinking that the spirit was gone. Suddenly "Uncle Sam" reappeared and stepped through the solid attic door! Jason repeated, "In the name of Jesus Christ, leave this house!" The spirit stopped in his tracks, turned around, and this time the attic door opened wide and "Uncle Sam" passed through. Behind him the door shut with a bang!

That afternoon Jason left out a letter to "Danny" asking him if he knew who this new spirit was. Around dusk "Danny" answered back: "DANNY DON'T NO GHOST". Within an hour, on the spread in the middle of our bed, we found a small note torn off a grocery reminder checklist. It read, "I'M LOOKING FOR MY BABY, I LOST HER!"

At last! Our first written communication with "Uncle Sam"! Lila and the boys noticed that the pictures were again starting to turn at right angles. Not all at once, but several frames were being turned a little at a time each time we walked by. The electric ceiling fan over the dining room was spinning at full tilt, and yet it was turned off at the wall switch! Our modern, brass chandelier began to swing back and forth so we stopped it and placed it in a neutral position, and then it started up swinging again in front of all of us! The lights of the kitchen began to flicker and the room seemed to darken then lighten a micro-second later.

Two more little notes appeared out of nowhere in front of us on the kitchen countertop! The same scratchy, non-descript blue ink writing as before was on each note. They read, "I FOUND HER! SHE IS RESTING UNDER YOUR HOUSE! I'M TAKING HER SPIRIT HOME, THANK YOU!" and "SHE IS THE ONLY ONE BURIED UNDER YOUR HOUSE, AND ONLY WE KNOW AND ONLY WE!"

Each circumstance that we faced this evening seemed to get more weird than the next. Jason spoke up and said to us, "Uncle Sam's" presence is around the house now and he has taken something back with him of little value!" "What could he mean, *of little value*?" I said to everyone there. It was just then that I looked down on the counter for the notes that "Uncle Sam" had written us, and they were gone! I asked him to return the notes to us that they were important and we wished to keep them. Within the next hour, the notes were back up on the kitchen countertop on top of the journals that I was keeping to record these supernatural events!

Uncle Sam's spirit writing to us acknowledging finding his lost baby under our house and taking her spirit home.

Chapter Three

It's Time to Call in the Parapsychologists

I contacted West Georgia College, which had on its staff one of the most notable parapsychologists in the United States. His name is Dr. William Roll. He had been the head of the Parapsychology department at Duke University, and is the author of many books on the paranormal.

One of his graduate students came to our house and interviewed each of us and sent a tape back to Dr. Roll, who in turn sent the tape on to Dr. Andrew Nichols, who is his close friend, and the director of The Florida Society For Parapsycological Research at the City College of Gainesville, Florida. Both of these esteemed gentlemen travel throughout the world studying cases of hauntings, ESP experiences, possession, psychic dreams, reincarnation, UFO'S, and psychic development, and they both lecture and hold seminars and workshops. They often travel together, investigating the supernatural for individuals and even governments.

Dr. Nichols arrived on an overcast, dreary day after driving five hours to see us to conduct an investigation into our poltergeist activity. He made us feel comfortable right away and told us to call him Andrew. He is a family man with children of his own, but he was giving up a Super Bowl weekend to come to see if he could help us with our problem. He talked to us as we sat around the kitchen table and gave us background on poltergeists in general. He even mentioned another family in Albany, New York, who had a somewhat similar case. Their poltergeist was writing on a chalkboard that hangs in their kitchen. This one was not writing kind messages, but, instead, swear words. Worse, and more frightening, it was driving knives into the walls. This family had a small baby and contacted Dr. Nichols when their baby had been levitated from his crib to their bed. Obviously, such behavior was a dangerous threat to the child.

Dr . Nichols spent two days going over our house from top to bottom with state of the art equipment. He told us that we have poltergeists that are intelligent and somewhat mischievous, but not dangerous. He did not witness anything personally, but gauged his assessment on the notes, photos, videos, and personal interviews that he had with each of us.

The readings that Dr. Nichols took in Jason's room at the north-east corner threw the meter off the scale! This same side of the room coincides with the wall to our foyer entranceway in our house. This is the side that we had originally

49

pressed the headboard of "Danny's" bed against.

The electromagnetic energy in that wall radiated over the bed and Jason. This may be the key reason to our meeting "Danny's" spirit since the bed was where he passed away in 1899 and his latent spirit was wakened by the energy from the wall. The spirit of the child woke and drew enough energy from Jason to move the toys around the room. Jason seems also more subject to seeing, hearing, and feeling "Danny," perhaps because of being bathed in the same electromagnetic field.

The terra cotta head that almost beaned Jason in the head a month earlier came zinging at him from this same wall. The electromagnetic energy didn't do Jason's little parakeet "Jacob" any good either, and he was found dead in the bottom of his cage early one morning as Jason was about to feed him. Jason was devastated and built a very nice memorial to the little bird in the corner of our yard. Jason had been feeling more tired than usual and this new information may well explain why. Every time these poltergeist entities wanted to move objects around the house they would simply feed off the energy of Jason and/or of the rest of us.

Another incident happened with our phone lines and those who were trying to get through to help us. Dr. Nichols spent two days at The Best Western Motel. When we were on the phone, all lines went dead at the motel and my house. Twice, the phones have gone completely dead, not including other forms of static interference that we observed. Once, someone rang the phone while we were all in opposite ends of the house. It ended its ring abruptly, and we all assumed that one of us had answered it. We found out later from the party who tried to reach us that when he called us someone had picked up the receiver but never said a word. We asked him if he was sure he had dialed the right number, and he said, "Yes, we could plainly hear and recognize all of you talking to each other, but when we tried to speak, all we got was dead air. None of us had picked up the phone during that time, and I can only attribute this particular incident to our poltergeists.

Lila ordered all the spirits to leave the house and told them all off. She said that she had had enough of their wrecking the peaceful stability of our household! This order for them to evacuate was said on the previous day to Dr. Nichols' visit. While he was interviewing the boys, Lila and I found another "Danny" note that was left back in Jason's room saying, "Why did you tell me to go?" She did not realize that by lumping all of our poltergeists together, she had inadvertently ordered both "Danny" and "Jill" away as well. She hurriedly wrote back to the little spirit with the hurt feelings a consoling note that read, "Danny, I didn't mean for you to leave; the other spirits were doing too many things! We do like 'Jill,' and I still have your Christmas present! LILA." We were still waiting for "Danny" to finish pulling the wrapping paper off of his gift, so we left it out under the tree and later on top of Jason's desk so he could find it and open it. "Danny" answered back "OKAY!"

It was nearly time for Dr. Nichols to leave and he went over his findings with us, saying that poltergeists seem to be staying at this point on a playful and friendly level, and they are intelligent and mischievous, but not dangerous. He added that when we all stay in a good mood they will tend to stay in a good mood also. He told us that these cases can last six months to two years or longer. Poltergeists will start winding down and get weaker and then just disappear altogether.

In his summation, he told us that we have a combination of "Poltergeist

Haunting and R.S.P.K." (Recurrent Spontaneous Psycho Kinesis)." Having twin fourteen-year old boys in puberty tends to draw these poltergeists because they can tap into our sons' energy. He asked me before he left if we could have some copies made of "Danny's" and "Uncle Sam's" writings, so I was glad to help him since he gave the kind of good advice that only a handful of people on earth are knowledgeable of. He also asked me if we had a tape recorder and, if not, he suggested that we should go pick one up for taping sounds in the house whenever we were away. Dr. Nichols said goodbye and headed down the drive.

I wondered what it must be like to travel around the world and investigate the supernatural, but I don't even have to leave my living room for that! I drove down to the "Big K" and bought a new General Electric tape recorder and tapes identical to the ones Dr. Nichols uses. When I got home, I made the suggestion that we all go downtown for a little antique outing and that we leave the tape recorder running while we were away. We left and came back home some two hours later. The tape had the usual air conditioner sounds as it turned on and off, but in the background we heard the sound of footsteps, a drawer squeaking open, a cough, and falling books!

Dr. William Roll had used a tape recorder during his investigation of the hold of "The Queen Mary," where, with incredible results, voices of sailors from the ship's past were picked up. The last few nights Lee had heard something scratching the screen of his outside window after dusk. I have heard some loud bumping and scraping and banging sounds coming from our attic. These are not the normal sounds that one might hear when a house is settling, but something beyond that. There has been a scraping sound over our roof which we plan to tape as well.

"Danny" opened his Christmas gift the following day on the desk in Jason's room. He wrote, "THANK YOU LILA!" and "I LOVE IT!" We wrapped a bisque figurine of a snowbaby holding stars over his head and a Beanie Baby Christmas bear. He had them sitting out in the shoebox that we had wrapped them in when we found them.

About this time, "Jill" started vying for our attention again. A spirit thrives on recognition and tends to grow stronger when noticed, but if you ignore it, it will grow weaker and cease to exist. Consequently, to get attention "Jill" moved her portrait again from the tea cart to the mantle, turned a painting sideways and, leaving a red ribbon on the frame, popped the clock case open and played with items in Lee's room.

Lee was really upset about "Jill" messing around with things in his room. So far she had dismantled a plastic/chrome perpetual motion art sculpture and left it in pieces under his bed. Sometimes she would put it back together and leave it spinning in the middle of his bed, and she has moved it all around his room from the floor, to a desk, to the top of his TV set. She removed a "Scream" movie costume from his closet and tossed it on the floor across the room. All his posters depicting skateboarding stars were switched from hanging on four sides of the room to spelling out "JILL's" name over his headboard wall. His room was visited by other unknown spirits as well, and they turned over pole lamps, turned his posters all at right angles, messed up his bed, took a quartz movement out of a clock, and made him feel unable to go to sleep because of the "eyes" he felt were staring at him.

Jason had a hard time with the unknown spirits staring at him, too, and they seemed twice as eerie when they chose not to communicate but continuously stared at him. Once on a cold, rainy grey Sunday afternoon, I laid down a few moments and fell fast asleep. On the other side of the house, Jason, who was also taking a siesta, was awakened by movement and sounds that were much louder than the thunder and lightning outside. He knocked at my door and I asked him what was going on now. He said, "Daddy, it's happening again; another spirit is in the house!" When I stepped out into the hallway, the first thing I noticed was that all the pictures were at right angles. When I walked into the kitchen the chandelier was beginning to slowly swing back and forth, so I told Jason to retreat to the bedroom and grab the video camera. We came back out and videoed the chandelier, which also had the bulbs and shades removed like once or twice before. On the dining room table, one of the shades of our stained glass lamps had been removed and left on the table end. Another lamp across the room had the finial screwed off and was about to be removed, but we interrupted the spirit in the process. A large chair that only seconds before when we had walked by had been upright was now lying on its back. "The Gone with the Wind" lamp in the foyer was disassembled. To top it all off, when I looked out the window, our house seemed to be the only one in the neighborhood without electricity. Unfortunately, just at this moment, the battery in our video camera died, so we lost the opportunity to catch more of this spirit in action.

Jason and I sat down at the dining room table and asked this spirit to communicate with us and let us know what he was doing there. In the kitchen, the stainless steel sink stopper launched itself like a missile out of the sink and across the room. It landed on the wooden floor with a loud "CLANG!" At this point, Jason said he could feel more than one spirit passing in the room. He felt the spirit of a young girl named Jessica Bradshaw and the presence of an older male spirit whose name began with a "Q." The impression that Jason received from the female spirit was that she had not cut off our electricity, but that the male spirit had. A chocolate foil-covered rose was lying on my bed and a happy face done in oranges and bananas was on the kitchen floor. I believe this female spirit was trying to make up to us for her companion's quirky deeds.

Lila and Lee came back from visiting at the hospital and were the first to find the fruit on the floor and ask me how it got there. Jason and I told them all that had happened at the house since they had been away. Lee was glad that he had missed these two unknown spirits and Lila was not ready to meet any other uninvited guests either.

It was "Jill's" turn to keep us on our toes and start attempting to get our attention. She started turning lights on at either the front or back door each evening around early night fall. She pulled Lila's electric curling iron from the bathroom drawer and plugged it into the wall because she had watched Lila do it many times and, I suppose, she wanted to emulate her. One night "Jill" opened our pantry door and took out chocolate chip cookies and poured two glasses of lemonade and left them out on the table at the back door for the boys. She left out her trademark red ribbon in the middle of the love seat to advertise that she was still with us. Lila had jokingly said that she thought "Jill" should start pulling some of her weight around the house and so she has.

Chapter Four

Jill, The Woman From The Portrait

Four days later, I was taking a nap on a peaceful Sunday afternoon when I heard drawers being opened in the kitchen dining room. No one was home at the time since Jennifer and Lee were off on a fishing expedition and Lila and Jason were out running errands for her brother, Edward. I walked into the kitchen dining area and noticed that the drawer to the secretary in the corner stood open. At first, I thought the house was just making odd, settling noises. Just a little more than the occasional run-of-the-mill creaks and popping sounds that houses make from time to time.

In about thirty minutes, Lila and Jason returned. The very first thing that Lila asked me was why I had set the Franciscan Apple pitcher and a bowl out on the card table in the foyer. I told her that I hadn't, and that they should have been on top of the mahogany china cabinet, where we always kept them. When we looked, we found Lila's senior class portrait on top of the china cabinet in their place. I was beginning to wonder if "Uncle Sam" had returned or if "Danny" were back. Is it possible that another spirit is about to make a debut?

That afternoon was filled with surprise after surprise, but I mean this in a very paranormal way. The house began to creak and groan, and we all looked up stared at each other wondering what in the heck was going on. Suddenly, the closet door in the foyer opened up in front of us. A gilt-framed antique oil painting of an Italian landscape swung downward on its bull dog hinges at a sharp right angle, making scratching noises like fingernails on a blackboard.

Poltergeist activity was running rampant all around us and we were all there to witness it together in the same room! Jason's room was being concentrated on the most now, as we heard an assortment of sounds emitting from his room. We walked back there to see what was up, and the room was dark, but we found two chairs were standing in the middle of his bed and a tee shirt from the movie *TITANIC* was hanging from his ceiling fan.

Twenty minutes later, the bumping and knocking sounds were coming from upstairs in the bonus room as the poltergeist continued to jerk us around one end of the house to the other. We climbed the stairs and found the mannequin's hands had been amputated from her arms and set on each arm of my Lazy Boy rocker. The left arm was on the left armrest, the right arm on the right. Even the jewelry she had been wearing on each arm was left in place.

We call the mannequin "Cynthia." Jason had expressed an interest in owning a mannequin several years before after seeing the movie's *Mannequin One* and *Mannequin Two*. We keep "Cynthia" upstairs guarding the wide-screen TV, and she is like one of the family. We asked that the spirit put poor "Cynthia's" hands back on and later we did find them back on but a little out of kilter. The upstairs bathroom light had been turned on, but the oval mirror was removed from the wall and set down on the floor.

More sounds were heard but this time they were downstairs in the kitchen pantry and the garage! Food was stacked up in one corner of the top shelf of the pantry when we opened the door. In the garage, toys and games had been stacked up on each other, and Jennifer's Strawberry Shortcake child's coat rack topped it off in the middle of the floor. Quirky stuff like this took place all afternoon as this new poltergeist was breaking us in.

Fifteen minutes later, Lila called me into the kitchen to tell me that while she was getting things out of the refrigerator and getting ready to cook dinner she placed the frying pan on the stove and turned around to get something else when the terra cotta angel appeared out of nowhere on the kitchen counter in front of her. While she explained this to me, I could see out of the corner of my eye the bathroom door slowly shutting by itself and I heard the door knob click!

The spirit Jill played a prank on us by removing the hands from a mannequin we call "Cynthia" and placing them on the arms of my recliner.

I thought I had a shot at catching our poltergeist in the act, but when I opened the door all the cabinets were opened and the floral arrangement that we keep on top of the toilet tank was delicately balanced on top of the bathroom ceiling lights! This was seconds after the door closed and no one was in or near the room but me.

Lila wrote "Danny" a note next and asked him to please tell us if he knew who this was. He said, "DANNY DON'T KNOW, SORRY." Lila was just a little more than agitated with these unseen spirits that kept passing through our house. There is a belief by certain people in Ireland that if you build your home over a fairy path, then your home will have disturbances until you remedy the situation by moving that part of the house where the disturbances occur or remodeling the house so that the front and back doors line up, leaving them open. Our disturbances occur all over the house, so I'm afraid remodeling won't remedy our situation. Oddly enough, the week's horoscope seemed to foretell our troubles: "Your house is the center of activity, which can get kind of frazzling. Might as well admit it, you wouldn't have it any other way. It looks like there is something amazing going on in your home." I clipped it out of the newspaper. Who says horoscopes can't sometimes shed light on your future?

That evening, just shortly before dinner, Jason and Lee were doing their homework at the kitchen table. Jason got up and was standing by Lila when he felt a cold rush of air pass behind him and the clock case in the living room popped open with a loud click. "I feel a female spirit is in our house!" he said. He walked back to the table and sat preparing to finish that night's school assignment when he was interrupted by a powerful chill down his neck and back. As he lifted his head, he felt compelled to look to the back of the house and then he saw her!

Framed beautifully by the hallway door, stood yet another spirit, this one a young woman who was dressed in a turn of the century white puffy-sleeved dress. Her brilliant blue and hauntingly beautiful eyes were staring right at Jason! She was fully materialized and wore her dark brown hair up in a bun. She wore large, gold earrings, and a long, gold necklace hung to her waist. He sat motionless in his chair, his eyes staring back into hers when she moved one step backwards into the hallway and faded into the darkness. Then he told us that the new poltergeist was a Victorian female in her early twenties!

The next four and a half hours were quiet, so we all went upstairs to watch a little TV and get our minds off our poltergeists. We had set out paper and pens in the usual manner in Jason's room and in the dining room, just in case our latest guest would like to sign in. At eleven o'clock precisely, Jason felt the same chill and received the same vibrations that he had earlier from the female spirit. "The young woman has written something downstairs!" he said. We all trooped downstairs and checked the dining room table first, but there was no note there. Then we checked the trunk at the foot of Jason's bed, but there was nothing. I was thinking this just might be a false alarm, but Jason was about to prove me wrong.

As we stepped into Lila's and my room, we saw a strange custom- made invitation standing up in the center of our bed. The large note-sized card had designs cut in the bottom and each edge was cut off like cards that were made in Victorian times. There was a neatly tied red ribbon at the base of the card. What an incredible way she had chosen to make herself known to us!

The invitation was hand-printed and read on the outside as follows: "MR. and MRS. COBB, YOU ARE INVITED!" The inside read, "WHEN: 12:00 p.m., DRESS: NICE WHERE: COBB HOUSE!" I showed the invitation to Lila, and we both couldn't believe what we were seeing, but here it was in our hands in red and black. I said, "Do you want to go? We may as well; we are already here!" She said, "I wouldn't miss it for the world!" We both then walked back to our bedroom to pick out our clothes for what was one of the strangest events of our twenty-five years of marriage!

Holding the fresh invitation from this new poltergeist in my hand, I walked out of our bedroom into the living room and found one of our china cabinet doors standing open. Napkins from the pantry and spoons from our kitchen drawer were somehow transported to the end of our dining room table! I began to feel an eerie coolness in the room and something suggested to my mind that we go upstairs after we dressed and wait for her to finish setting the table.

I wished I could be in the room to video tape the poltergeist in action. I whispered into Lee's ear to take our new video camera and set it up downstairs on the kitchen counter and aim it at the dining room table. This could be the break we had been waiting for—to capture a genuine poltergeist on film! Lee did as I asked and joined us back upstairs until twelve o'clock a.m.

The grandfather clock downstairs was chiming twelve times as the four of us walked downstairs to attend the "Spirit Party." As we headed down the staircase, Lila told me her head was buzzing and she felt as if she were coming down with a migraine. I felt a flutter of butterflies in my stomach and experienced a rapid heart beat. Lee was a bit nervous and fidgety. Jason stood right beside us in a semi-trance-like state. Jason's mind was picking up classical music playing, and visualizing hundreds of people dancing around us! I felt a keen sense of light breezes touching my face and hands.

Jason was living the actual phenomenon by seeing and hearing and feeling this party and describing it to his mother and me! "The lady that I saw in the hallway is sitting in the love seat and drinking tea!" he said, as he pointed directly in front of Lila and me. I could see an indentation in the pillow on one end of the love seat, but I did not see what caused it to press inward. "Don't you see her?" "No, Jason, I can't," I said. Next Jason told us to look on the table. I asked him what it was on the table besides the napkins and the spoons that hadn't moved since we had gone upstairs an hour earlier. "There is food of all kinds piled high in sterling silver bowls and serving trays!" he said, astonished that neither Lila nor Lee or I could see it. "I know you are truly having a second sight on this party, Jason." " Continue to tell us all that you see."

Jason went on to describe the people who were waltzing in costumes from at least one hundred years before. They almost seemed to be from an old movie playing and re-playing one of the happiest times of their lives. He told us they were not just within the confines of our home but all around the outside as well, and as they danced they would pass through our walls and continue to waltz with the music.

I took a photograph of an area in the room that I sensed movement and when I played it back on my camera I had captured a glowing spirit ball floating behind the four of us! The video camera had done the strangest thing. It had somehow managed to lock itself down and turn itself off! This is the type of camera that you have to manually turn off! When we played back the little bit of footage that the camera did take, we discovered a white wisp of smoke that looked like a lightning bolt and then the sound of the camera turning off!

The party seemed to break down after I took a shot with my digital camera, but Jason could still see the woman on the love seat talking with another female spirit while enjoying a cup of hot tea, although the second woman's face was a bit blurry and the sounds of the party began to quiet down. We were all very tired this evening, so we turned out the lights and retired.

One hour and a half later, Lila woke me up out of a sound sleep and told me she heard noises coming from the dining room again. She had sat up so quickly that it startled me and I left our bedroom to investigate. I saw that all the chairs in the dining room had been reconfigured into what can only be described as an attempt to widen the ballroom floor. They were pushed back against the walls so the phantom dancers could sit and socialize with one another! There were even four chairs over near the foyer where Jason had told us the sound of the band came from! I checked on the boys and both were sound asleep! It looks like the party continued on without us!

The following afternoon a red Christmas candle that we had out on the dining room table self-combusted before the eyes of the three of them when they arrived home from Chucky Cheese. The light was acting very strange and flickering and dancing as if some unseen force was fanning it. Lila walked over and blew out the candle and challenged the spirit to light it again. All the air and fans were off, so they couldn't explain why the flame leaped and danced as it had, but at a little past ten that night Lee found the candle had re-lit.

Two days later I picked up Jason from school. Lee had taken the school bus home earlier so he was resting upstairs when we arrived home. Lee said he wasn't feeling well and that he rather not go out to dinner with us, and I said that it was okay. Jason and I washed up in the downstairs bathroom by their bedroom and left for the mall. We didn't get half way down the driveway when Lee raced out of the house in front of us with his arms flailing. "We've not been out of the house a minute, now what?" I said to myself.

"They're back," and you should see our bathroom!" Lee said excitedly as Jason and I pulled the car forward and parked in front of the garage. Inside, the boy's bathroom had been the victim of poltergeist activity again! The light bulbs and shades had been removed, the drawers all pulled out. A framed print was turned at a right angle and the flower arrangement on the top of the toilet tank was balanced on two of the bathroom ceiling lights again! Lee told us the very second we shut the front door that he started hearing the bumping and pounding sounds that we had all previously experienced, so he didn't want to be home alone and raced outside to get us! The Franciscan Apple pitcher was moved from the top of the china cabinet to a lamp table as well! I decided to call Lila at work and report this to her. She told us to stay home with Lee, and she would bring home a bucket of chicken for dinner.

I returned to my home from work the following day with an old water-stained watercolor of a Victorian woman. I had bought her for one dollar at a yard sale some two or three months before. I had been thinking to myself that the woman spirit that Jason had described in the hallway and at the party was suddenly very familiar to me. I had laid this old portrait down on the floor of the upstairs corner of my shop and she never sold. I felt inspired to take her home and let Jason take a look at her. I put her in the trunk of my Volvo and drove home. Jason and Lee were standing on the sidewalk when I pulled up. I called Jason's name and motioned for him to come over and see what I had in the trunk of my car. His eyes widened as I lifted the trunk and he saw the portrait for the first time. "That's her!" he said. "Where did you get her?" I repeated the story of how I ran across her at a yard sale when he suddenly said, "Her name is Jill." If you take off this old worn frame you will find her name on the back of the picture!" he matter-of-factly added.

After I removed the old paper on the back and next the old frame, I took the portrait out and studied the reverse and found the name "JILL." The writing was in a very light pencil and barely discernible, but there. Jill's eyes were the kind that can easily follow you around the room. I left her out of the frame and lying on her back in the dining room that night when we went to bed.

The following morning when we got up the portrait was missing! We found her on the mantle in front of another yard sale find I had made twenty years before. That was an antique gilded portrait of a mother and son, circa 1880. Lila tells me that she is getting a mental imprint that "Jill" wants her portrait restored. Later that evening while we were standing in the kitchen the drawer under our kitchen sink slowly opened in front of us! The other china cabinet in the living popped open too! Lila quickly shut them back, but in a few moments they had opened up again! Thirty minutes later I was missing the red invitation that "Jill" had given us to her party. It was spirited right out of the journal notebook I was keeping! Jason said that "Jill" had taken it back because she had felt slighted by the fact that neither Lila nor I could see her at the party and only Jason could. Thank God that I had the sense to video tape it or no one would believe us that it actually existed! We never got the invitation back even though we asked "Jill" to return it. Jason said that she had already destroyed it and that that was the end of that story.

Jason is still hearing that waltz playing in our house as if the party still continues and the tape plays and replays over and over. "Jill" is becoming something on the order of "Danny" as she writes to us about things relating to the family. We had a talk with Lee about his school work and other personal problems including our poltergeists and their affect on him. Lila, at this point, prefers to have them leave and has told them so out loud! "Jill" left out two messages of which one was directed at Lee. It read, "LEE TELL MOM AND DAD TRUTH, YOU ARE A GOOD BOY!" The bottom note was to Lila and me. It read, "SORRY AL AND LILA, WE WILL LEAVE, GREAT PARTY!, JILL." For some unknown reason, "Jill" does not want anyone to hang on to her communications, so on the reverse of this one she wrote, "PLEASE DESTROY THIS AFTER READING, PLEASE! 'JILL'" and she followed with her symbol of a heart with an arrow in the center heading upwards.

Her second note read, "AL, THATS A HORRIBLE PICTURE OF ME I THINK." I asked Lila if we should keep them and she advised me to do what "Jill" said and destroy them. I couldn't make myself destroy them and I gave them back to Lila who slipped them under the old gilt wooden frame that "Jill's" original portrait was found in. Moments later, she peeked under the frame and the notes were gone. Her sister Vickie did not know the notes had disappeared but was amazed when Lila lifted the frame and they had vanished into thin air.

Chapter Five

Multiple Spririts Find Our House Through The Portal

Ever since Dr. Nichols helped us pinpoint the "Portal" in the hallway wall, we have been visited by many other spirits both named and unnamed. The energy that seems to radiate from the wall acts as a doorway that draws these entities into our home. They seem to pass through this tear in time and space and can enter our dimension as if through a swinging door.

Our first thoughts about who could be leading them to us was "Danny." He made himself at home right away and visited whether or not his bed was here. Spirits do communicate between themselves as was proved to us in an earlier episode with "Danny" and "Little Gracie Watson." Many of these spirits were seen and felt by Jason, Lee, and our little dog, Lady. Sometimes they have partially materialized with just a head and shoulders passing by. Other times, they made themselves known by causing a rush of cool air as they invisibly moved passed us. More than twice the boys have seen strange men dressed in old fashioned hats and coats strolling down the hallway. They seem to prefer disappearing into the laundry room or our bedroom.

On the evening of March 23, 1999 we returned home from dinner and a soccer match to find the house in pitch darkness. Both boys remembered leaving inside lights and porch lights on for our dog, Lady. Lila and I almost tripped over Lady as we stepped through the threshold and found her shivering all over. Once inside, we cut the lights on to find the house had been visited yet again by spirits unknown.

The house had been in clean and neat condition when we left together some three hours earlier, but now it was a mess. A man or something seemed to be under our bedspread, but it was only the covers lumped together, even though the bed had been freshly made when we left the house earlier that evening. At the end of our hallway, a picture was turned at a right angle and the laundry basket was spilled over. A little wooden carving of a naked man in a barrel on top of my highboy was tossed down to the floor. Things were jumbled around our house, objects moved that were impossible for our little dog to reach.

Over time, we have developed the habit of keeping the house tidy so that we can document with film what things have been moved by the poltergeists. We continue to put up with these phenomena because we feel no eminent danger from the poltergeists, but Jason constantly reminds us that he feels we are being watched all the time. The eyes on him make it difficult for him to fall asleep at night, so he tries to block them out of his mind, eventually falling to sleep.

The following day the very same thing happened to the hallway and laundry room. The moment that Lee and Jason got home from school they could hear the loud raps and banging coming from the attic upstairs, so they called Lila at work and held the phone so she too could hear the sounds. The boys walked upstairs and saw Jason's mannequin move her head and they feared she may start to walk toward them next. Downstairs our room was a wreck! The mattress and bedcovers were turned at a ninety degree angle, and the pillows and sheets were hanging off each end. A chair that Lila and I hang our clothes across was pitched forward on its face and the contents scattered all over the floor. An antique pastel seascape was turned at a right angle like all the other paintings and prints in the house have been found. There may be something to the fact these pictures and prints are all turned at right angles. Perhaps they are used by spirits as entrance and exit points.

We called out and asked these prankster spirits to leave. This time we told "Danny" and "Jill" that we knew it wasn't their style and that they could stay. I told my mother and my sisters about the bizarre occurrences that have taken place in the house and they are justified in their fears about coming to visit us. That evening "Danny" wrote a note saying, "AL DON'T TELL YOUR MOM FLORENCE OR ROBIN OR KATHY ABOUT ME, OKAY." He continued, "ANY OTHER SPRITE (SPIRIT) BECAUSE THEY ARE SCARED OF US!, OKAY AL, AL, AL "DANNY." I know that he felt he was responsible in some way for keeping our family separated, and he was remorseful. They have been finding excuses not to make the three hour drive to our house for a year and a half.

In some respects, "Danny's" feelings are well-grounded. Many people are indeed afraid of the unknown and are fearful that anything outside of our own world could exist. "Danny" was the first "other worlder" to make his presence known to us and in so doing has changed our lives forever. I know that we will come to no harm and the experts in the paranormal have told us that these spirits are good. We continue to believe that God is watching over us daily and our guardian angels have kept the evil spirits at bay. The following Friday night "Jill" decided it was her turn to liven up the house. She made the room feel cooler than normal and proceeded to open all the kitchen cabinets. Next, she opened two china cabinet doors in the living room, including the Larkin Soap premium desk that I purchased for Lila on our first anniversary in 1975. The GWTW lamps at both the front and the back door came on without our help and a pair of red candles were burning at the end of the dining table. She must have been party mood that evening.

Moreover, despite the lack of rain during the previous week, water appeared in the fountain in the front yard. "Jill" also continued to drive Lee crazy moving his things around the room and playing with the little plastic chrome perpetual art sculpture by taking it off track when he wanted it on or on track when he wanted it left alone.

At 9:00 p.m. the following evening I was speaking to Dr. Nichols on the phone and giving him an update on our poltergeist activity. Jason was passing Lee's room and found all of his posters spelling out "Jill's" name and she had started up the art sculpture again. Dr. Nichols was amazed that these poltergeists had remained active for so long and planned right away to make a second visit to our home as soon as he could get in touch with Dr. William Roll, his associate.

The next day I took the family out to eat since I don't cook. I still had some shopping to attend to at the mall, so Lila and the boys came home after meeting me earlier for dinner. Jason put on his track suit and running shoes and Lila and Lee followed him on their bikes. They rounded a few blocks in the neighborhood when Jason decided to run back to the house and get his bike and join them. He stopped at the refrigerator to get a cool glass of water when he noticed the sounds of the ceiling cracking and the attic sounded as if a herd of buffalo were stomping about. He began receiving strong mental images that many spirits were wandering upstairs and downstairs and he heard the sounds of every couch and chair creaking as if under the weight of invisible bodies. He felt their presence overwhelming and turned around to leave as quickly as possible to warn Lila and Lee that we had more company.

The first thing that they noticed when they arrived on their bikes was a blue folding beach chair that was sitting by the open garage door. It was in the same place that Lila's father used to sit outside and smoke his cigarettes when he visited us for dinner when he was alive. A plastic lawn daisy windmill was also found spinning in the back yard. It, too, had belonged to Lila's dad and he had it in his back yard to scare off ground moles from his garden. It was a small momento from her dad's house that Lila had put up in the garage. How did it find its way outside when no one had planted it in the ground?

The following night I returned home from a Savannah Stamp Club meeting to find a little shoehorn back scratcher that I had upstairs had been dismantled and laid up on the couch on the opposite side of the room. They are constantly pulling pranks or maybe it's just a spiritual curiosity to see what makes things tick. Electric plugs have been pulled from the walls on several occasions, but no real serious hazards have taken place except for the curling iron being taken out of the bathroom drawer and left on.

Over the next few days, Lila, Jason and I all heard the kitchen trash can lid open and close over and over, so I thought Jason's brother, Lee, was playing games. I called downstairs but did not get an answer. I investigated a few moments later and found the boy was nowhere near the kitchen and had been working on his class homework assignment. He told us he had heard a disturbance in the kitchen too but assumed it was one of us. Jason walked back to his bedroom to work on his homework and flew right back out holding his leg and telling me that something had burned him! I examined his leg and found a red welt the size of a pencil eraser! We were never able to explain how that came to be and nothing of that nature has happened since. The stopper in the kitchen sink made a "whoosh" sound and popped out of the drain hole for the second time! This time Lee, Jason, and I saw it fly across the room and bounce on the wooden floor not far from where it had landed previously. Lee spotted a dark shadow of a man moving behind us and I kept waiting for another crazy thing to happen. I did not sleep well that evening as I kept my eyes open most of the night guarding, I suppose, against whatever dark figure Lee had seen.

Chapter Six

Walter's Arrival In Mid-April 1999

The boys and I were shooting baskets and working up a sweat in the driveway on a pleasant April afternoon after I came home from work. Jason said, "I'm thirsty, Dad. I think I need to go inside and get a soda." "Fine son," I said. "Go ahead. Your brother and I will finish our game of horse." Jason pulled a soda from the ice box and was pouring it into a glass of ice when he heard the muffled sounds of something jumping on the bed in our master bedroom. He first thought that Lady, our dog, might be up on our bed again. He realized that we had just purchased a new bedroom suite and that this bed was set far higher than our previous suite, so Lady could not possibly get on it.

Jason peered into our bedroom and could not believe his eyes. The black and white panda that Lila owned as a child was running and bouncing on our bed! The stuffed bear jumped to the tall mahogany bedpost and spun around it like a fireman slides down a pole to a fire.

The bear's plastic eyes were rolling in their little toy sockets, and the mouth was opening and closing quite differently from the frozen smile the bear usually sported. The bear made a high-pitched baby sound much like a giggling Pokemon creature or a Teletubie Baby. Jason raced out of the room to get Lee and me so that we could witness this latest quirkiness.

Jason said, "Come quick. It's in your bedroom!" Lee and I charged through the kitchen and down the short hall to the bedroom with Jason directly behind us. I rushed into the room and spotted the black and white panda bear on top of my highboy with his eyes still spinning. I knew where the bear had been sitting when we left to play basketball earlier. We left him up there and the boys and I returned to our game of basketball.

Once outside the boys filled me in on what may have led up to this latest event. When they arrived home from school, they had gone in my room and found the light on in the closet, but the door was shut. The panda was sitting straight up with its back to the bedpost, facing the door when they walked in. When I left for work that morning, I had definitely cut off the closet light and left the door halfway open. There was no bear on the foot of the bed. Lila keeps that bear out of harm's way on the top shelf at the rear of the closet. Pleasant childhood memories have instilled in her the need to preserve the bear in good condition.

The panda bear was still at the foot of the bed when I came home that afternoon so I told the boys we would leave him there to show their mom when she got off work. Then the boys and I went outside to shoot some hoops. I thought that "Danny" had been responsible since he was "the toy horse" and had played in every room in our house, including the attic.

We were traveling down Montgomery Crossroads. heading east towards Ryan's Steakhouse when Jason told me that the impression he is receiving is that this spirit is not "Danny," but that of an elderly man, a man who, in life, was a professional puppeteer! I had no way of knowing what strange event would challenge us when we sat at our kitchen table an hour later.

I was bringing my journal up-to-date and writing about this latest episode with the panda bear when Jason began to channel the thoughts of this spirit of the elderly man. Jason had a very strange gaze and glint in his eyes as if in a hypnotic state. I sensed that I wasn't talking to Jason now but to the spirit he was channelling. I asked the spirit, "Who are you?" "My name is Walter Greenfield," the spirit answered. "When were you born?" I continued. "I was born in 1864 and died in 1948, just two months and two days before my eighty-fifth birthday." The spirit went on and told me as he continued to use Jason as his conduit that he lived in Michigan and had died at home in his bed of a respiratory illness.

In life, the spirit of Walter Greenfield told us, he loved antiques and had collected gold twenty dollar pieces known as double eagles. He said his occupation was that of a vaudeville performer, who travelled the big city circuit. His biggest regret was having a very special custom-made puppet stolen from him and that he died before he could ever recover him. He went into great detail describing this puppet as having real glass eyes and a monocle similar to the famous "Charlie McCarthy." He had a special gold-lined carrying case made for him that has dry-rotted since the theft many years ago. I asked him why he had come to Savannah, Georgia, to search for this puppet, and he said his spirit had traced the destination to Savannah. His spirit soul will not rest in peace till we can locate this puppet. Since I attend all the local auctions and estate sales, "Walter's" spirit thinks I will be his ticket to finding this lost relic. I told him I would try to help him in this quest. He told me how relieved he was for our help and he left Jason's body. I found Lila's black and white panda at the center of our headboard later that evening to remind me to keep my word to "Walter."

Chapter Seven

Danny Shows Us What A Creative Poltergeist Can Do

On the eighteenth of April, 1999, my family and I saw an ad for a southern plantation house for sale in the Sunday edition of the *Savannah Morning News*. The house was part of a larger plantation that had existed since the 1860's, and it was now for sale in Oliver, Georgia. Oliver is a beautiful, rural community in Screven County, just 45 minutes outside of Savannah, Georgia. We made an appointment for the following afternoon and arrived about an hour early. We spent that time just two hundred yards down from the plantation house that we had come to see, and, while there, we admired a beautiful Baptist Church that had been standing there since 1790. I brought along my digital camera and we photographed the old family cemetery that stood behind the church.

The time flew by very quickly and we drove back down the road to the beautiful plantation house we came to see. We were met at the door by a very gracious lady, who showed us each and every room that were filled with southern antiques and collectibles from the Civil War era. We loved the house and lush green pastures that surrounded it. The plantation is known as "Willow Bend" and was settled in the early 1860's. General Sherman stayed on the grounds near this area in December of 1864 before capturing Savannah, Georgia, and presenting the city as a Christmas gift to President Abraham Lincoln on December 25, 1864.

My family and I enjoyed Mrs. McCabe's tour and history lesson of the grand house. It would have been a done deal for us to live there, but too far for Lila and I to commute to work each day. Lee and Jason both admired the mansion and grounds as well, but we had to face reality. We drove home, all of us dreaming that we wished the plantation was located closer to Savannah.

We had only been back home a few minutes when I walked into the master bedroom and found an internet sheet I had pulled off the computer prior to our visit that morning about the "Willow Bend" plantation house. The internet sheet was surrounded by other sheets that I recognized as being in little Danny's handwriting, which said: "AL, AL, AL, Please Rethink House," "Danny (NO) About House," and "If You Don't Buy House To Live In Buy For Investment_____ Danny". On the reverse of these letter of plea, "Danny" added, "Danny, Jill, Walter and Spirits Know About House" and "Please! Please!"

On Monday, Lila was on the telephone with her sister Vickie Ledlow when Jason walked into the bedroom and interrupted their conversation by telling Lila that a man was at the front door. Lila hastily told Vickie goodbye and went to answer the door, but no one was there! Jason told her that he had seen a tall, older man in a top hat and long coat and tails standing at the front door. He was holding an invitation of some sort wrapped in red ribbon, but Lila did not see him although she did hear the door bell ring. Lila opened the door and walked outside and down the sidewalk to the end of our long drive, but she never saw the mysterious caller. He had disappeared into thin air! Lila got a chill down her back that something was about to happen and she knew by women's intuition that it would take place very soon!

The spirits had used this clever diversion to get both Lila and Jason away from the master bedroom, so "Danny" could leave another message and lay it out on our bed. This time "Danny" had written in brown Crayola crayon on nine separate sheets of notebook paper. The sheets read as follows: "Al, Lila", "Al, Al,"...."Al, Lila"...."Al, Lila"...."Al, Lila"....."AL"..."Lila"...."Lila, AL", ... "Time Is Running Out!!!!" "Danny" had written on the reverse of the last note, "Hey Lila, Buy The House!"

Jason and I were sitting at the kitchen table later that afternoon when we both heard the sound of children's wooden blocks banging together upstairs. We both knew that no one was upstairs at that moment. Jason looked at me and confirmed that he sensed "Danny's" presence playing upstairs with the red, green, yellow and blue building blocks that I gave him and his brother when they were small. We patiently waited till Jason could no longer feel "Danny's" presence in the house, and we both climbed the stairs to investigate.

On the floor upstairs, in front of the large picture window, "Danny" had spelled out his name by laying out the blocks flatly and in a very creative manner. I also noticed that "Danny" made an arrow pointing to his name: "Danny By House." I grabbed the digital camera and the Polaroid and photographed this event and saved all the notes "Danny" ever wrote to us. I recommend that if you ever encounter a strange and unusual situation such as ours that you document everything going on for future study.

Two days later, Jason and Lee arrived home after school and heard "Danny" upstairs again playing with the blocks. When they went upstairs to investigate, they found that "Danny" had built an exact replica, as well as you could build one with the toy blocks, of the "Willow Bend" plantation, complete with the fountain out front just as we had seen it on Sunday!

"Danny" left a message to Jason that all of the spirits in our house had travelled with us to see the plantation in Oliver, Georgia, and that they all wanted us to move there where they will co-exist with us! "Danny" further stated that it is just like the "two story mansion" that he grew up in North Carolina and that he missed it so much that Jason could hear him crying.

While Lee and Jason were both upstairs looking at this latest incident, "Danny" was in Lila's and my bedroom. Spread out over the full length of our bed, "Danny" had taken a roll of "Witch Stichery" brand dress makers hemming tape from Lila's sewing box located in our bedroom closet and used the entire roll of it, laying out the framework of the "Willow Bend" plantation. From the sewing box, he also borrowed a small pair of scissors and proceeded to cut up a cracker box from our kitchen pantry from which he made the "gingerbread" woodwork on the plantation house. "Danny" used yellow Easter basket filler for the roof and added some of "Lady's" dog food and filbert nuts for further decoration. He topped off this masterpiece with two tiny die cast metal plants from a shelf in our kitchen to complete the front yard! Another note accompanied this art work, saying "By House, AL, Lila!" The boys had passed our room only moments before, investigating the sound of "Danny" playing with the blocks. All this took place while they were upstairs in a few moments and neither heard anything going on downstairs!

Later that same evening after Jason and Lee had gone to bed, Lila and I found a note pinned to the wall at the foot of the stairs so that we could not possibly miss it. He was still pushing us in his spiritual way to buy the plantation! Talk about persistence. "Danny" wins first prize hands down!

This is what it is like to live daily when you are open to and accept the fact that poltergeists do exist and can communicate with you. I know when I go home tonight that something even more strange and unusual is just over the horizon. I recently found a shiny, new 2000 Sacajawea gold dollar lying sideways on the highboy in my room, and no one knows how it got there! I know that I'm now on an adventure of a lifetime and I can never look at things the same way again but overall it's been enjoyable.

Danny is very persuasive

66

Chapter Eight

The Unfriendly Spirits

On April 29th, 1999, we could feel a heavy, unfriendly atmosphere developing around our house. One could feel that something wasn't right and it felt as if we were waiting for the other shoe to drop. Both Lee and Jason complained to me that they felt an eerie presence that we had never experienced before. That night, each felt that eyes were staring at them and their homework. For four straight evenings, a group of malevolent poltergeists tore the bedcovers from our bed and flipped all our paintings, watercolors, and prints at right angles. The bedposts' wooden finials were removed from each of the four posters and the center finial was taken off the center of the headboard. A small lady's Queen Anne armchair had been pushed face down on the floor with clothes scattered everywhere on each of the nights.

The strangest thing in the room that the poltergeists seemed to despise the most was a wooden figure of a naked man in a barrel that had a trick spring-loaded penis that would fly up when anyone lifted the barrel over his head. This gem was bought at a yard sale and brought home and placed on top of my highboy. I never thought I would have a problem leaving it on the highboy, but every night for four straight nights, it was thrown across the room and bounced off the wall. Who would have suspected that a harmless tourist item made in Jamaica would set these spirits off. The spirits found the poor, wooden man in the barrel the following day in the drawer where Lila had hidden him and broke off both his arms and his penis!

We prayed to God to send these low-level poltergeists away. They continued to harass us by unscrewing light bulbs and shades and tipping over chairs, frightening our dog, and making a general nuisance of themselves. The worst damage they did was to unscrew four, 120 volt, high intensity bulbs from our ceiling fan and throw them with such force against the wall, they exploded and left deep scars in the walls' surface.

On our bed one evening, we found a note written on computer paper from our upstairs printer that said: "WE ARE NEVER GOING TO LEAVE!!!!! STUPIDS!!!!" The printer upstairs, I might add, was not in working order when this message was printed out. We prayed once again for these evil spirits to take a hike. Thankfully, the house quieted down for the rest of the night.

One other evening, I came home and the boys showed me what the poltergeists had done, creating a mess around the house. "Your momma's going to have a fit," I told them. So we cleaned up the mess and went outside to play basketball. After twenty minutes, we came back inside to find everything rifled through again.

On the final night of the series of freak poltergeist activity, Jason came home alone from school since Lee had makeup work to do. As he shut our front door behind him, he heard the house let out a groan and the sound of footsteps running up the stairs. He scooped up Lady the moment she ran up to him, her body shaking in absolute terror!

Doors and cabinets made sounds as they opened and closed, but Jason continued to investigate further into the house! In Lila's and my room, he found two knives sticking in the ceiling over our bed with a threatening message attached. The message was filled with profanity and expletives, demanding that we leave the house immediately.

Jason read the letter hanging down from the ceiling and then turned quickly and ran to the kitchen phone to call Lila at work. Frantic, she told him to leave the house at once. Jason hung up the phone and bent down to pick up Lady and headed for the front door. No sooner had he closed the solid wooden door behind him that he heard a loud thud. He did not know until later when we opened the front door that he had narrowly missed being stabbed in the back with a steak knife! The knife was deeply embedded in the door at the chest-high level. Jason was indeed very lucky that he left with Lady when he did.

This was the most serious incident of the dark kind that we had ever been involved with. We asked Lila's sister Vickie to have the church pray for us in their next prayer circle since the power of prayer is the greatest power on earth. God thankfully answered us. We no longer have this group of malevolent spirits trespassing and causing chaos in our home. Miraculously, they simply melted away.

My family and I have learned a great deal about the supernatural world of the poltergeist these last thirteen months. The world of the poltergeist has not been fully explored and there is much that we can learn about them. I don't believe we have even scratched the surface in hearing all we can about these paranormal creatures. We have been fortunate in some respects to have made contact with "our friendly poltergeist spirits."

Journal Entry

May 31st, 1999: *1:10 a.m. Lila and I hadn't been in bed for an hour when Jason knocked at our door and sleepily asked us to step into the living room with him. We were shocked to find his bed, mattress, pillows, and covers had been transported to the living room in front of the fireplace! Lady, too, had been removed from the bedroom with her bed! She was visibly shaking but remained by Jason's side.*

Jason is not subject to sleep -walking and is a very deep sleeper. Lila and I would have certainly heard the disturbance that would have occurred if anyone were rearranging the bedroom and the living room in the dark. Possibly the only answer I can attribute to this mystery is the fact that we have been searching for a replacement bed for Jason since we sold Danny's bed last October. This has been weighing heavily on Jason's mind these past few months and I believe his psychokinetic abilities kicked in while he was asleep and transported him into the living room.

I photographed the living room and Jason's bedroom and then Lila and I helped move everything back into Jason's room. We had to turn the bed sideways to get it to go through the narrow hallway door. I got up three or four times to check on Jason during the long night, but he stayed in a deep state of sleep and Lila and I listened for any other disturbances, but nothing else took place.

Scientists are still studying the effects of PK and the human mind. There are so many other facets of our mind that need to be sharpened and used. We need to learn so much more about God's gift to us, our minds.

Chapter Nine

June 1999 Update

"**D**anny" still flits in and out of our home at less than a moment's notice. Recently, he left a little message on Jason's bed, written on the notebook paper we always leave out for him to write to us.

Jason," he wrote, "Tell lady she did not by me. She bought bed. Stupid Lady!" "Danny" tends to vent his anger with us concerning each new owner of his bed. Everyone who has ever owned it bought it with the intention that "Danny" would come forth and move objects for them as well.

It is true that "Danny" visits the bed from time to time to check on it, and he is well aware of all the new owners, but as he stated in his note, "She did not by me!"

This June has been fairly quiet on the visitation-of-the-spirit front. Last night I found that "Danny" had taken a note I had written to myself concerning what type of home I would like to move to next. I had laid this sheet of paper on Lila's dresser after we discussed my ideas. I found my list of ideas on the dining room table with another sheet of paper next to it.

"Danny" had written "Danny Like Idea!" in red-colored pencil and placed an arrow in the left-hand margin pointing at my list. Things have quieted down a good bit over the last month since our interview with *48 Hours*. Both Lee and Jason have felt cold spots in the house, and each of them has seen a tall male apparition walking through our house and disappearing down both our hallway and theirs.

One night Jason sat upright in his bed and looked across the hall to Lee's bedroom and saw a strange multi-colored spectre getting up out of Lee's bed with Lee sound asleep beside it. Jason's wall paper seemed to come alive one night and bulge outward as if something were crawling under it, and it moved counter clockwise until it reached the closet and then disappeared. Shadows fleeting across the walls and hallways have been acknowledged by Lila and the boys.

It is hard for a sensitive child such as Jason to have to block the constant feeling of eyes on him all the time, eyes which seem to monitor his every move. And, then, he has to come to grips with the impression that these disembodied spirits wish to speak with him. He literally has to close them off or he would not be able to sleep at night.

Even Lady, our pet dog, is affected by all this paranormal activity in our home. She often jumps from her basket with her ears pricked in a straight-up fashion, listening to sounds in the attic or downstairs. She will freeze in one position, much like a hunting dog on point. She also sees the spirits and barks and, sometimes, snaps at them if she deems them threatening.

City of Savannah Department of Cemeteries

330 Bonaventure Road, Savannah, GA 31404   (912) 651-6843

March 23, 1999

RE: Lot 98, Section E, Bonaventure Cemetery

To whom it may concern:

The referenced cemetery lot in Bonaventure Cemetery, Savannah was purchased by W. J. Watson on April 22, 1889. The Department of Cemeteries is not aware of any legal descendants of the lot owner on record. In the absence of a lot owner or heir, the Department of Cemeteries has authorized Al Cobb to photograph the John Waltz sculpture of Gracie Watson on the referenced lot and to use the photograph on the cover of a book, "They're Here . . ."

Sincerely,

Jerry Flemming,
Director

Letter authorizing use of Gracie Watson for book cover.

    Lee is still experiencing a scratching on his window screen at night, and we have never been able to spot anyone outside his window when it happens. I have also heard a scratching sound above me on our roof which is also unexplainable.

    Because of these experiences, I have become more interested in the supernatural. This past weekend, the Searcher's, which is a group that investigates paranormal experiences, Lila, and Jason and I met at the Colonial Cemetery on Abercorn Street and Oglethorpe Ave. in Savannah, Ga. The dusk was slipping away on little cat feet as a light drizzle came down on our little group. We came prepared to photograph and video tape whatever would come to the surface to meet us.

    Within the two hours that Lila, Jason, and I stayed, I took thirty-four digital photographs. The first was an interesting picture of the back wall of the cemetery breaking back to the left. In the distance, one can see what appears to be a stark white shape of a face staring out from the center of the tree at about ten feet high.

Another fascinating photo was my eighth shot, which showed Billy Barrett walking away from me with his video camera in tow. Billy recently joined The Searcher's and is now an avid ghost hunter. The amazing thing about the shot I took of Billy was the bright blue aura that I captured on his left shoulder. The aura was very unusual, and it looked like a hand had been placed on his shoulders with fingers pointing outwards.

A really amazing thing that often happens when photographing in a cemetery is that batteries seem to give out or die even though they may be fresh. My flash failed to work when we approached the mass graves of the yellow fever victims of 1820 grave-site. Another member in our party, Beth Ronberg, had a dickens of a time getting her film loaded in a manual camera. Many of my shots came out completely dark, even though I was near street lamps and light poles in the cemetery.

Kathy Thomas, the founder of our Searcher's Club, had difficulties with her camera flash as well. Overall, we all had a good time and even learned more about the cemetery's history.

Perhaps, these paranormal events are tied to the history of the region. During the occupation of Savannah by the Union soldiers stationed here in the winter of 1864, the bored troops had nothing better to do than desecrate the graves in Colonial Cemetery. Some of them carved on the headstones different months and years that they thought would be funny or nonsensical. Since the winter chill was getting to some of them, they opened up most of the vaults and cast out the corpses and slept in them. They quartered their horses there and generally grave robbed and vandalized the whole cemetery. It took many years until the Department of Parks and Trees came along and made the cemetery what it is today.

Whatever the case, my family's experiences with the paranormal are by no means the only ones in the area.

Journal Entries

Sunday, July 4th 1999: Poltergeist Update
Today was bright and sunny and turned out to be a firecracker of an Independence Day! I took Lee with me for a little fishing on the Frank Downing Bridge. Lila and Jason chose to stay home and work in the yard. When Lee and I returned four hours later, Lila pulled me aside in the driveway and told us that while we were gone, a ventriloquist dummy I let Jason take home, was found in the chair in the foyer instead of the chair in the living room where they had left it before they went out into the yard! It was a 1970's model "Danny O'Day" with an impish grin on his face.

All Lee and Jason could think about was the evil "Chuckie" doll seen in horror films, and they asked me to take him back to the shop. I took him back to the shop the next day and as far as I know he has quit wandering around during the day.

Wednesday July 7th 1999
It's my night to cook so I took Lila and the boys over to the Loop Restaurant in Chatham Plaza for a little pizza and hamburgers. When Lee and I returned, we didn't notice anything unusual in the kitchen. Lila and Jason came home just five minutes behind us and when they walked into the kitchen they noticed the strange event.

Two perfectly fresh Green Granny Smith apples in a basket sat on the kitchen counter in front of them, and Jason decided to have one for desert when he noticed it had changed! The apple no longer had that perfect unblemished shine to it. As Jason held it, he showed his mom that something incredible had happened to it as they stared at the change in total amazement! The apple had been sliced completely up, down, and around the apple's circumference as if done by a surgeon's hand!

I know Jason has two very sharp Exacto blades that he uses in his fine arts classes, so I asked him where they were. He went to look for them but only found one of them in an upstairs closet where he keeps his art supplies. He came back downstairs a few moments later with a perplexed look on his face. Although he had never used these Exacto blades, the one he found had a darkened tip on the blade as if it had been placed in an open fire and the second blade was missing and has never been found since!

Thursday July 8th 1999
The second Granny Smith apple remained in the basket. We froze the first one after I photographed it. Before I took the family out to the Oglethorpe Mall for dinner this evening, I examined the apple and it was fresh and had a nice shiny texture with no bumps or cuts in its surface what-so-ever. I spoke out loud for the spirit who had cut the apple the night before to come back and cut on this one. I

laid the apple back down in the basket, and we all went out the door together. In the meantime, I locked the door behind us. I was the last person to see and touch the apple we left behind in the basket.

On our return from the mall, I was the first one in the house and I made a bee line for the basket on the kitchen counter. I wasn't disappointed; the spirit had three small vertical cuts in the apple! I checked the tip of the burned end Exacto blade that we had left on the kitchen table and, sure enough, it had a small drop of apple juice on the edge of the blade!

There is no chance for teen trickery in this experiment since Lila and I were with the boys the whole time. There are some things that still go unexplained. Later the same evening, our phone rang once then stopped. I thought Lila had picked it up downstairs and she thought I answered it upstairs. In fact, the party who called us said they could hear the TV's playing, but no one answered the phone! Now, it seems our phone calls are being intercepted!

is not the first time the spirits played around with our electricity. The lights have been cut on and off both at the box in the garage and on individual lamps in the house! Several times when on the phone, our messages have become garbled and the phones have gone dead at home and at both my office and Lila's.

August 5th 1999
Last night we had a meeting of our club and went on to investigate a private home owned by Ben Farmer on Modena Island. Ben, his wife Julie, and their housekeeper Cleo have seen unexplained spirits and shadows on the estate. We concluded our visit around 11:30.
The following day at 3:25 p.m. Jason called me from the house and said, "Dad the ghosts are back!"; then the phone went dead! I drove home as soon as possible. Upon my arrival at 4:00 p.m., I found both Jason and Lee standing in the driveway in front of the garage. It takes a lot to frighten these two boys, who along with their mother and me have witnessed many strange occurrences in our home the last eleven months!

"Don't go in the house, Dad!" they said.

Jason showed me a tiny pin prick cut, although he could not remember how it had happened. They both witnessed a steak knife fly across the kitchen floor and an umbrella shoot out of the laundry room and bounce off a clothes basket sitting on the floor! A putty scrapper also skidded across the kitchen floor and landed in the corner under a tea cart!
When I entered the kitchen, I could hear some movement and cracking sounds in the upstairs bonus room! The blade of the steak knife was protruding out from under the partially open pantry door. The umbrella laid in the hallway. A record book and pens and pencils were also scattered on the floor!

One of the first things that was most evident was the wood mullions that had been pulled out from each and every window in the house, including the bathrooms and

74

garage, but excluding Jason's room. The curtains had been pulled down in several rooms as well. The colorful framed prints leading upstairs had once again been turned sideways on the wall, but this time it was different! They were turned right then left, then right and left again. Before, they had always been turned at right angles only. The top of the stairs were barricaded with four chairs and an oak swivel rocker. On the floor, spelled out with colored blocks, was the word "VICTORY " and a two story house was built behind it!

A necklace had been ripped off the mannequin that stands upstairs and tossed on the green loveseat in front of her. As I walked back downstairs, I saw the dining chairs had been switched with the kitchen chairs, and pictures in the living room had been alternated from wall to wall. Lila's mahogany child's desk was moved from the foyer to the living room. Both Lee and Jason's bed covers had been pulled back as if something had slept on them.

I brought out my tape recorder and spoke with both boys while the incident was still fresh in their minds. Jason told me that he had taped the front door open as he was putting on a coat of new paint when the tape ripped from the floor and the door slammed in his face; the door locked, and the key fell out onto the inside foyer floor!

Lee was riding his bike in front of the house when he looked up into the upstairs bonus room window and watched some invisible being pulling out the window mullions one by one! When the two of them went into the house, they both witnessed the steak knife, the putty knife and the umbrella flying across the house.

Lila's sister Vicky came over and blessed the doors and windows of our home. We also said prayers together and individually to keep these low-level harassing spirits away.

August 9th 1999
Our pet poodle, Lady, seemed to sense something happening downstairs as she suddenly leapt out of her basket and laid on the floor at the feet of the mannequin we call "Cynthia." She lay quite still with her ears prickled in an upright listening position facing the steps leading downstairs.

Lila called Jason and me from upstairs and asked if either one of us had moved her mother's framed picture to the card table in the foyer and turned on the lion-faced "Gone With The Wind" Lamp? No one had, and we had all been together in different parts of the house when Lila realized it had been moved. No explanation was found again and we retired for the night.

Chapter Ten

The Haunting of The Benjamin J. Wilson House

Just after the "War of Northern Aggression" (1861-1865), a businessman named Benjamin J. Wilson moved to Savannah and built a gorgeous sixteen-room, two story house in 1868. It is located at 432 Abercorn Street and is bordered by East Wayne on the North and East Gordon on the south with a pleasant view of Calhoun Square and the historic Massie school (1856-1974) in the front.

The spacious home has its original 1868 period hardware and has fourteen-foot crown-molded ceilings. The mirrors over the mantle came from another Savannah icon, "The Pink House." The bar is reported to have belonged to President William McKinley. The first floor parlor doors have stained glass as beautiful and original as any found in the entire city of Savannah. The present owner has been in the process of restoration for a number of years.

On the side of the building is a fine, gated garden area leading outward to East Gordon Street and above the garden are two beautiful verandas decorated with outstanding ironwork comprised of oak and acorns entwined.

Flash back twenty-six years to 1973. David Gabriel, his wife Janora and their two children, David (22) and Lisa (18), have just moved into the Benjamin J. Wilson House. Young Lisa, a fellow Savannah Christian classmate of mine (I graduated in the class of 1972) had been given the first floor parlor bedroom at the back of the house. All went well for a short time until Lisa was awakened one night at midnight and witnessed glowing balls of light that appeared to be made of fire moving around the room.

The very walls of her room seemed to come to life and a stream of liquid ooze crept across and down the wall from her bed where she was sleeping. This was the first time she had ever seen ghostly ectoplasm and had no idea what the source was. She raced out of the room and slept on the couch until the sun rose. She went back into her room, but the strange ectoplasm had disappeared. Lisa was sensitive to the unworldly vibrations that the house was telegraphing to her senses.

Lisa's mother, Janora, also had some rather hair-raising experiences take place in front of her in the house. One time she witnessed a young woman who fully materialized in the house and was heading up the spiral staircase with her back turned to her. The spirit was wearing an early American dress and sun bonnet that looked to be a working class outfit, but it was made of a shimmering white and brown calico material. The lady went halfway up the stairway and then dis-

76

appeared.

On another occasion, Janora found many heavy boxes of books that had been moved from one end of the long hallway to the other. She found two large wing-back chairs lying on their backs and other furniture that had been moved around while they were in the house and away from the house.

David Gabriel tells me that they moved after a little over a year, but their moving had nothing to do with the poltergeists that seemed to constantly tease them. They all look back and remember the strange occurrences that took place in 1973.

Flash forward to July 15, 1999. My son Jason and I drove to the historic district in downtown Savannah so I could show him my latest ghost story project, the Benjamin J. Wilson House. We parked on the North side of the house on East Wayne Street at 8:00 a.m. The previous day on one of my morning walks I had passed by the house and I was overcome by the strangest feeling that told me this house is spirit-filled. Jason was excited with anticipation that we might well encounter another spirit. The current owner told me over the telephone that she has never experienced any spirits in the house since she has owned it.

As I was pointing out to Jason the fine quality of the original stained glass double doors, he jumped back and said to me, "Dad! I've just seen a woman in a shimmering white dress pass by the door in front of us!" I had not previously mentioned to him the woman spirit that Janora Gabriel had described to me.

He told me he feels this woman spirit was a good spirit, who normally keeps to herself, but this time she was just curious as to who we were and why we were standing on her front porch steps.

I quickly fired off my camera into the open mail slot and managed to capture a misty image of a spirit on the spiral staircase. I had no way of knowing that I had succeeded in getting a ghost shot, but I was pleasantly surprised when an additional shot showed a ghostly mist coming from the top of the parlor doorway. On further research, we had found that a young man committed suicide upstairs above Lisa's room in the 1940's. Lisa also told me that a gentle male spirit liked to caress her hair as she lay down in her room.

The spirit, as far as we know, has not been seen by anyone in the last twenty-six years since Janora Gabriel saw her in 1973, and now Jason Cobb and myself in 1999. The Benjamin J. Wilson House is still haunted to this very day and we have photographic evidence to prove it!

Chapter Eleven

The Phantom Children on Jefferson Street

At Nine North Jefferson Street at the corner of Williamsom is a fine antique warehouse called "Jere's Antiques." Jerry Myers started the business in 1976 with his dad, Ronald Myers. Jere's dad was a friendly fellow who passed away on June 8, 1990, and Jere has continued running the business since then. When I interviewed Jere, I asked him in all the thousands of pieces of furniture he has ever handled if he ever had any paranormal or unusual things happen in his massive warehouse. He told me the following story that was first brought to his attention by an employee named Bill Harris.

As part of his business, Jere receives container loads of antique English furniture every month, and he carries the most impressive inventory of old furniture of any dealer in Savannah, Georgia. His historical building was a cotton warehouse built in 1882. The building has a long history that it could tell if only walls could talk

On one occasion in 1981-1982, Jere received an English five piece bedroom set, and he had Bill Harris and several helpers move it upstairs to the second floor. Within a short time, Bill and the other employees, whenever they were downstairs, heard the sounds of running feet across the floor boards on the second floor. When they would investigate the sounds, they found no one there. The sounds of children's voices laughing and playing filtered downstairs and were heard by Jere and his employees. Again, when the second floor was investigated, the voices ceased and no one was ever seen. The paranormal activity seemed to center around the antique English bedroom suite

Bill would often comment to Jere that "those kids are upstairs playing again, Jere. Can you hear them?" Jere confirmed to me that he has heard the children as well. Since Jere has sold the antique English bedroom suite, the children no longer haunt the second floor of the old cotton warehouse. Jere told me that he hasn't had another paranormal experience with any antique furniture since then.

Chapter Twelve

"Old Joe" at St. John's Episcopal Rectory

In the very heart of the historic district of Savannah stands the greatest example of Gothic Revival architecture built in the South. The building is well known to everyone as the Green-Meldrim House located on beautiful Madison Square.

The architect for this splendid mansion was Mr. John S. Norris of New York City. The quality of Mr. Norris' designs was simply incredible. Not only did he design the Green-Meldrim House but the Champion-McAlpin House, The Customs House, and the Andrew Lowe House, as well as many other fine structures during his stay in Savannah from 1846-1851.

The first owner of the residence was an English businessman named Charles Green, who came to Savannah to seek his fortune in 1833. By the early 1850's, through wise investments in the cotton market and by being a prominent ship owner and trader, he amassed a large sum of money and, coupled with his business connections in England, he built the mansion for $93,000.00.

Mr. Green's ships carried most of the building materials directly from England as ballast. But still, records indicate the basic building materials were in the $40,000.00 range and that was in 1850 period dollars! That same home built today would exceed $4,000,000.00.

The son of Charles Green, Mr. Edward Moon Green, inherited the estate in 1881. In July 14,1892, the year of the Columbian Exposition, Judge Peter W. Meldrim purchased the house for his residence until the Meldrim family sold it to the St. John's Episcopal Church on December 30, 1943.

The Green-Meldrim House became a National Historic Landmark in 1976. General William Tecumseh Sherman used this very house as his headquarters during the occupation of Savannah by Union forces in December 1864.

Since 1943, The St.John's Episcopal Church has converted the former stable, kitchens, and servant quarters into the rectory of the church. The Reverend Ernest Risley, then rector of St. John's, was the first to stay in the new parish house. He would listen to classical music and play the piano and the harpsichord

He noticed that whenever he was alone a door would quietly open by itself. Since Rev. Risley's time, there have been several paranormal occurrences in the rectory. The current reverend, Rev. William H. Ralston Jr., tells me that the old black servant of Judge Peter Meldrim and his wife Frances is actively haunting the rectory. He was a black man, and his name was "Old Joe."

He would tap his feet to the music as he entered the room to serve refreshments to the Meldrim party guests. He is remembered by past family members as a music lover and he would always smile broadly and enjoy the party as much as the invited guests. The footsteps Joe makes as he crosses the old floorboards of the rectory can still be heard as he moves from one room to the next. Of late, he still makes his presence known by pulling on the purses of ladies as they pass through the rectory on tour. Rev. William H. Ralston Jr. seems to be convinced that since he has been in the process of moving out of the rectory, "Old Joe" is a bit upset since he hasn't heard the music he loves lately. He may have stayed earthbound since he loved and cared for the house for so many happy years.

Chapter Thirteen

An Afterlife Experience In Paradise Park

Several years after Jim Tillman's father, Walter, died, the Tillman household, Jim Tillman and his wife Caroline, had a very interesting visit. It was an ordinary evening at #4 Paddy Circle in the quiet subdivision known as Paradise Park in Savannah, Georgia. Jim, an employee of the Coca-Cola bottling plant, had just finished supper and was relaxing in a comfortable recliner, enjoying a favorite television program. Suddenly, a strange and strong feeling came over him, and the room's temperature seemed to drop by several degrees. He felt as though someone were standing close behind him, looking over his shoulder. Quickly, he turned his head and caught the image of his deceased father standing in the room with him. His dad was wearing the same green khaki pants and white shirt that he always wore at the J. B. Williams Gulf Service Center that once had existed on the corner of White Bluff and Montgomery Crossroads. His dad smiled reassuringly as Jim did a double take and wiped his eyes, not believing what he was seeing. He no more than blinked twice before the ghost of his father had disappeared!

That same evening, Jim's wife, Caroline, was busy down the hall in the laundry room, ironing. She, too, saw Jim's dad's ghost standing in the hallway and smiling at her while she worked. The image was brief and fleeting, but she noted the event in her mind yet at the time she refrained from telling Jim what she had seen.

Several days passed and Jim decided to tell Caroline that he had seen his dad just a few nights prior. She looked at him funnily and acknowledged that she, too, had seen the apparition in the hallway on the same evening! She asked Jim if his father had been wearing his Gulf Service station uniform, and somewhat in disbelief Jim confirmed what he also had seen. "Was he wearing the black hat, too?" she asked. "Yes, he was," Jim said.

No other sightings of Walter Tillman have taken place since, but, sometimes, between two and three a.m., when Jim's dad used to arise to have an ice-cream sandwich, smoke a cigarette, and get ready for work, Jim and Caroline have heard the distinct sound of the old ice box opening. Even though the old ice box sits outside and is no longer plugged in or in use, Jim's dad's spirit still remains to continue his old habits.

Chapter Fourteen

A Story of Life After Love

The world of the supernatural is not confined to only one plane of existence. We all as living beings are subject to the life forces that surround all of us. Both the seen and the unseen worlds are intermingled in the universe we all live in. Some people are more gifted than others in feeling the presence of these spirits around them. For some, these presences are indicated by be a sudden change in the temperature, causing goose bumps to break out on the surface of the skin. For others, it is a buzzing sound in their inner ear as spirits try to communicate with them.

I have experienced these spirits manifesting themselves to me and my family by moving objects and leaving written communication in the form of letters and notes.

The forthcoming true story is a tale of spirit communication after death. The names have been changed in some instances, but the facts remain the same. The mid-1980's was a busy and prosperous time for Johnny Quest, a young Savannah building contractor, and his wife, Natalie. They lived in a fine home that Johnny had built at 306 Jackson Blvd. in the Jackson woods subdivision in Savannah, Georgia.

Johnny was on the go at all times and had many projects he was working on completing. One major project was the building later to be named for him on Professional Plaza Blvd. Even a young, healthy, individual can burn the candle on too many ends, and soon the stress took a tragic toll on Johnny's body. One night he suffered a massive heart attack and choked to death in his sleep. Natalie had no idea what was to soon transpire the night after her husband's death.

Natalie was in a deep sleep when Johnny came to her and stood at the foot of her bed. He told her that he was in a better place and was not in any pain. He also said he had never felt as good nor been as happy, ever. Before his image disappeared, he told Natalie to go on with her life and be happy and he would always be around to protect her.

Cleo Taylor worked for Johnny and Natalie, and later after Mr. Quest's death, she cleaned the offices in the completed office building now named in his honor. Cleo had the habit of locking herself in the building while she cleaned the offices. One night, while all alone on duty, she heard doors slamming and footsteps walking down the dark corridor. She called Natalie at home and told her she thought someone was in the building with her. Natalie told her not to be afraid and that the sounds she was hearing was only Johnny making sure that his building was being maintained. Cleo had one confrontation with Mr. Quest's ghost one evening as she was depositing that day's trash in the dumpster on the side of the building. He appeared to rise up from the ground in front of her and stared at her momentarily in a friendly manner. Cleo froze in her tracks, unable to move or say anything, to the white-suited spirit in front of her. In a moment he turned his head toward the building and took a few steps and disappeared through the wall! Cleo told me during our interview that she has never had a supernatural experience before this incident with Mr. Johnny. She is a member of St. Peter's A. M. E. Church and knows that it is possible for spirits to exist. After all, isn't The Holy Ghost a spirit?

Another witness to the disturbances in the Johnny Quest building was former tenant, Richard Goreman, who tells me that many sounds were heard when he was alone in the building in his office after 9:00 p.m., finishing up paperwork. He confirms what Cleo Taylor heard since footsteps and slamming doors took place late at night when he was locked in alone. He left his office to investigate several times but never saw anything. But he did, he said, feel an odd presence of someone watching him in one of the dark corners of the building.

Natalie continued with her life very much aware that Johnny remained with her. In a couple of years she met Ben Farmer, who became the new love of her life. Ben and Natalie moved in with each other and were engaged to be married. They lived in the Modina Island home that Natalie designed, and Ben had built.

Ben is a prominent Savannah Real Estate Broker and active in many Savannah community projects. When Natalie moved in with Ben, little did he know that she had brought with her the bed that Johnny Quest had died in. When he first lay on the bed, Ben began to experience heavy breathing on his neck and an overpowering sensation that he was being watched. Early one morning, Natalie had gotten up to use the powder room, and Ben was violently punched in his side. Some powerful force grabbed both of Ben's arms and pulled them forward trying to jerk him out of the bed! Ben screamed out to Natalie to come and wake him out of the nightmare he thought he was having! Next, the television set came to life on its own and chills ran down both Ben's and Natalie's backs.

Ben asked Natalie what was up with the bed and that's when she told him that it had been Johnny's. Ben gave the bed away to his son to take to his dorm at Georgia Southern University, but that didn't last long. Only a short time after he gave the bed to his son, he got a phone call. It was his son on the other end asking him if he minded if he returned the bed. Something was breathing on his neck when he slept on it at school. Ben felt chills run down his back again! This time he contacted his job foreman, Bill Lyons, who knew a psychic in South Carolina who might help them. Bill carried a photograph of Ben Farmer with him to show the psychic. The psychic was named Marian Stearns who was well known in the low country for her talent. The moment that Marian touched the photograph she had a burning sensation come over her and immediately told Bill to have Ben come and see her as soon as possible for it was extremely important.

When Ben met with Marian Stearns, she warned him of a terrible car crash that he may be soon involved in and that he may be trapped and burned to death. He avoided the future tragedy by getting rid of his red sports car that she had envisioned him dying in.

Later, when Marian Stearns met with Ben and Natalie, she confirmed to both of them that Johnny's presence was in the room with them and that she could see Johnny's arms around the shoulders of Natalie. She added that Johnny was earthbound and was moving back and forth between the physical and the spiritual planes. She advised that they travel back home to Savannah and get in touch with a medium who could help Johnny get to the other side and not remain earthbound.

Another psychic/medium came to Savannah from Hilton Head, South Carolina, and performed an exorcism to free Johnny and send him into the light. Other spirits, this time American Indians on the island asked if they could be allowed to pass through the doorway that the psychic had created. The psychic said it would be all right after he first sent Johnny on his way. The Indians followed, some ten or twelve in number.

Ben and Natalie later went different ways, and Ben remained at the isolated Modina Island by himself and his two dogs. It took a little while for Ben to get used to being alone. There were few houses on Modina in the beginning and spaced far apart. Ben's house is on the far northern tip of the island. Neither of Ben's two dogs, the German Shepard nor the Pit Bull, would go upstairs by themselves under any circumstances. The feeling of being watched began to over take Ben's normal life, and he began to wear a pistol every where he went on the island. The same feeling he had before caused anxiety to set in and Ben added an additional lighting and alarm system to the house. It wasn't possible for him to shake off the feeling of danger to his safety. To this day, he feels the presence of something, although he cannot explain what it is, but only that it's eerie.

Cleo Taylor now takes care of Ben's and his new bride Julie's house on Modina Island a couple of days a week. She recently spotted the figure of a dark, headless spirit standing in the corner as she was loading the dish washer. Julie has seen American Indians in tribal robes walking along their dock in the twilight mists at dusk.

The land that Modina Island sits on is the site of Pre-Columbian Indians that lived and died there some two thousand years ago. The early Indian mounds indicate that the area around Ben's house and the opposite end of the island was used as a sacred burial ground. The ancient Indians fished the river and hunted the land long before any European set foot in America. The Indian spirits up to now have allowed the settlers to stay as long as they do not desecrate the sacred burial grounds, and these spirits are still active today.

Chapter Fifteen

Elaine

It's 1976, and the American Bi-Centennial celebration is in full swing. The two hundred year-old mark of American independence is cause for national pride in God and country. Danielle Rossiter and her husband, Jimmy, and their five-year-old daughter, Wesley, moved into their new home in the Henderson tract of Isle Of Hope in southeast Savannah, Georgia. Everything was going well and Danielle and Jimmy were enjoying the house and the new neighborhood.

One day Danielle came into the house and smelled a strange acrid burning odor, and she quickly ran into the kitchen and made sure the oven wasn't left on. She checked the iron in the laundry room as well. The acrid burning smell was still permeating the air. It was very disturbing to her that she could not pinpoint the source of the odor. She could not explain the odor, but she could feel a bone-chilling cool spot as she walked through the nursery room where little Wesley slept.

Danielle seemed to sense that there was a presence in the room, but she could not explain who or what seemed to follow her all around the house. She enjoyed doing her nails as she watched television and often brought the nail polish and remover from the bedroom to the living room. She repeatedly found the nail polish back on her dresser in the bedroom when she knew she had just carried it to the living room. On many occasions the lights in the house would independently turn themselves on and off. The toilets sometimes flushed by themselves, and books were moved all over the house, even with no one around. This seemed to happen quite frequently, but Danielle and Jimmy got used to this strange phenomena.

Three years later they were blessed with another baby girl, named Linda. Each girl had her own bedroom until little Linda was able to talk and tell her mommy that she was scared to stay alone in the nursery anymore. Danielle moved Linda into Wesley's room to help her daughter feel safer and sleep better. As Danielle passed by the girl's room one day, she could hear them both talking to a new girl friend. She assumed they had made a new friend in the neighborhood and stuck her head in the door to meet and greet the child. There was no child there. The girls were seeing and speaking to a little girl, called "Elaine" about their age who told them she had passed away from the yellow fever epidemic back in 1820.

"Elaine" communicated to both the girls by telepathy and they could see her materialize in her early-American period dress that she had died in. The girls played and interacted together as all children do and treated "Elaine" as another sister. Danielle soon saw "Elaine" materialize in front of her after she learned that her daughters had a spirit for a playmate

Danielle described "Elaine" as having long, dark curly locks flowing over her shoulders. She wore a long, white gown that dropped down to her feet. The material was almost transparent and flowed like a butterfly's wings. These visitations continued to happen throughout the time the girls were growing up.

Years later, when Danielle and Jimmy's marriage was in trouble and the two of them would argue and fight, their disagreements would upset the girls and "Elaine" as well. "Elaine" began to react to the stress in the house by slamming doors and knocking things off shelves and breaking them. She also kicked and knocked around the girls' book bags in her anger over the family situation.

Dannielle told me that one day she cut off the ceiling fan while the girls were off at school and Jimmy was at work and she heard a little voice behind her say, "Why did you do that?" This was the only time she had ever heard "Elaine" speak out loud.

Danielle and Jimmy were having another fierce argument in their bedroom when they both heard something heavy bounce off the end of the bed! "What was that?!" Jimmy exclaimed. Not long after this strange incident, the girls called Danielle to come to their room quickly and when she charged in she witnessed what the girls were excited about. A guitar that was propped up against the wall was strumming itself as if invisible fingers were playing a strange melody.

Nineteen years later, Wesley returned to the house to visit her father. Danielle and Jimmy had long since divorced and Jimmy still lived in the house. "Elaine" let Wesley know that she was still a presence in the house by turning the bathroom light back on after Wesley had just turned it off before leaving the house. Jimmy was unavailable for comment, but Danielle and the girls are sure that "Elaine's" spirit remains in the house to this very day.

Chapter Sixteen

Other Haunted Furniture
Discovered in Savannah

Many pieces of antique furniture have been known to retain the imprints of their previous owners. So many, in fact, that several books have been written on haunted furniture. Somehow, certain furnishings from the past are able to repeat or record past experiences of the people who once owned them and, much to the awe of present-day owners, they play these scenarios back. Spirits have been known to inhabit wardrobes, tables, beds, desks, chairs, and even candlesticks and the like.

Such inhabitations of furniture are not uncommon here in Savannah as well. Recently, at a local auction house in Savannah, a consigned antique mirror that was hanging on the wall suddenly began to shake. The mirror was witnessed by three of the auction house staff who told me they couldn't believe that an inanimate object could try to shake itself down from the wall, something this mirror almost succeeded in doing. The mirror finally stopped on its own accord and was sold to a local buyer who has had no problem since he hung it in his home.

On another occasion, a long-time antiques dealer and friend purchased an antique American low boy and placed it in his shop. Within a few months, he noticed several items in his shop were constantly being misplaced. He knows the location and provenance of all his shop inventory. He had strong feelings that he wasn't alone and he finally called out to whomever it was to leave him alone and return all the items that were missing.

Within a couple of weeks, everything was returned to him in the general areas that they were removed from. He got the impression that it was the spirit of a woman who haunted his shop, although he never saw her materialize. He thanked her for bringing back all the important items he had been missing.

A major antiques show was coming up and he decided to take the low boy with him. It was among the first items sold and was delivered to the new owner, a young woman.

When he got back to his shop, everything seemed a little different. He did not feel as if he were being watched anymore. The following six months were peaceful and uneventful.

Six months later, he was exhibiting at a show in the same city, and the young lady came to his booth.

"Sir," she stated, "I have a bone to pick with you!"

"Do you remember the antique American lowboy you sold my husband and me six months ago?" "Of course I do, is there a problem, he replied." "Yes, ever since it was delivered to our house the tv and stereo have been turned on in the middle of the night!"

My friend calmly told her, "Maam, you have bought yourself a ghost, and as my sign says, all sales final, no returns, no exchanges, no refunds."

Summary

The world as we know it is in a constant state of evolution, revolution, and change psychologically, idealistically, physically, politically and, perhaps most of all, spiritually. Are there genuine haunted houses? The evidence is factual and overwhelming that they indeed exist. Our world today is filled with many people who are sensitive to the thoughts and feelings of spirits who have passed on and returned to communicate important messages to friends and families. They can channel these thoughts through the living and take care of unfinished business they had when they walked the earth. Are these spirits, poltergeists, and ghosts directed by the devil? Only rarely, does the devil use them for his work. God's creatures are in all forms of life and afterlife. The power of God always supersedes anything the Devil can throw at Him. Most spirits are benign in nature and readily able to communicate with the living if they are open to them.

The vast majority of people do not realize that ghosts and spirits walk among us daily. We are often communicated with by spirits in our dreams and in a thousand other significant and insignificant ways but fail to heed whatever messages are left us. You must remain open-minded about the supernatural. The financial pressures of day-to-day life and hectic schedules thrust on us all can make it difficult to accept that there are invisible beings trying to speak to us. It seems like a fairy tale to be fortunate enough to have communicated with these spirits as my family and I have. I wondered what "special" ability we had over everyone else that this should happen to us, that we should warrant a visitation from the other side. I have always considered myself as just plain folk, but this I do know: these spirits are looking to communicate with ordinary people as they once were.

"Faith" is what all Christian religion is based on. My faith in God has been greatly enhanced by the interaction my family and I experienced with the spirits and poltergeists. Just having a message travel to you from the other side is an awesome experience. It is the initial communication of the third kind, seeing, meeting, and understanding something that you had only read existed.

Spiritualism will gain its hold on all mankind in these upcoming years of the new millennium. This will us all lead into a cleaner, purer, and more thoughtful world than has ever existed since the Garden of Eden. The teachings of our Lord, Jesus Christ, will ring as true in the future as they did in his day.

These little, invisible spirit-helpers and entities have co-existed with mankind since the early dawn of time. The next thousand years will find us all in some form of mass communication with God and one another as never before. All this supernatural knowledge will not only be global but inter-dimensional as well, including all living souls from the dawn of time that God has breathed eternal life into.

The earth will live in total harmony, and future generations will be adept at the unconditional love of God and respect for all God's creatures and creation. Then, all demons will long since be cast out into oblivion, since God no longer will have a need to test mankind and sin will be non-existent. It will then be, as it indeed is now, truly only God's universe.

In writing the stories in this book, I hoped to bring you, dear reader, to the realization that we are not alone in the universe, but many of us are not even alone in our own kitchens. I have included only a few of the stories of other Savannahians who have had paranormal occurrences in their homes. They came forward with their stories to me because they knew I would not laugh at them nor disbelieve their tales of the supernatural. This book has been focused on the spirits, ghosts, and poltergeists who have made themselves known in Savannah, Georgia. There are many more stories to tell about the spirits who weave themselves into the fabric of everyday life all over the deep South.

Our time here on earth is but a learning experience. We are all placed here to go through a series of "Life Lessons". These "Life Lessons" will benefit us after we have "crossed over" into "Summerland." From cradle to grave, we all must strive to learn from life's ups and downs. Each of us chooses the paths we will walk daily to learn another "Life Lesson." The souls of all mankind are interlinked, and we all share the same responsibility for our "soul growth" and that of our brother's and sister's "soul growth."

All God's creatures that he has breathed the "life spirit" into are eternal and have souls. Our dearly departed pets that we have loved and lost will be waiting for us when we also "cross over."

Our supernatural experience with "Danny" proved to my family and me that beyond a shadow of a doubt that there is a "Summerland" waiting for all of us, filled with love, hope, and beauty to be shared with friends and family. For now, however, our spirit guides and angel guardians watch over us and guide us in our daily "earthbound schooling."

We must all continue to keep an open mind and our individual spirit guides and angels will upon occasion mentally tap into our thoughts and validate their approval of our advancement through "life's lessons." This is their way of letting us know that they are walking beside us and supporting our continual learning process.

I have been contacted by both my father and my in-laws who have "crossed over" in the last fifteen years. They have reached me and communicated with me through my dreams. They have all told me that they are fine now and doing well on the other side. This contact has further validated my belief in all the life-after-death theories I have ever been taught. God has created a "learning plan" for all of us long before we are laid in the arms of our parents. "Life lesson #1" began for us at our birth and it was a major ongoing "life lesson" for our parents. God's ultimate plan and purpose for all souls can be summed up in one word: "LOVE."

Bibliography

Calhoun, Mary. *While I Sleep*. New York, New York: Morrow Junior Books, 1992.

Manning, Matthew. *The Link*. Vale, Guernsey: Colin Smythe Limited, Gerrds Cross, 1987.

Scott, Sir Walter. *The Waverly Novels*, "Kenilworth." New York, New York: Thomas P. Crowell & Company, 1890's.